AMOUR AMOUR

Amour
Amour

ANDREAS EMBIRICOS

Translated from the Greek
by Nikos Stangos and Alan Ross

*

MASTERWORKS OF FICTION (1960)

GREEN INTEGER
KØBENHAVN & LOS ANGELES
2003

GREEN INTEGER BOOKS
Edited by Per Bregne
København/Los Angeles

Distributed in the United States by Consortium Book Sales and Distribution
1045 Westgate Drive, Suite 90
Saint Paul, Minnesota 55114-1065

(323) 857-1115 / http://www.greeninteger.com

First American Edition 2003
English language translation ©1966 by Alan Ross
Published in translation originally as *Amour Amour* by Alan Ross (London: 1966)
translated by Nikos Stangos and Alan Ross
Published in Greece as *Grapta* (Athens: Agra, 1960)
Published by permission of Agra through agreement with
Imrie & Dervis Literary Agency, London
Back cover ©2003 by Green Integer

This book was published, in part, through a grant from the
Center of Greek Books, EKEBI. The publisher would
to thank the Center and the original publisher, Alan Ross.

Design: Per Bregne
Typography: Kim Silva
Photograph: Andreas Embiricos

LIBRARY OF CONGRESS CATALOGING IN PUBLICATION DATA
Andreas Embiricos [1901]
Amour Amour
ISBN: 1-931243-26-3
p. cm — Green Integer 87
I. Title II.Series III. Translators

Green Integer books are published for Douglas Messerli
Printed in the United States of America on acid-free paper.

CONTENTS

INTRODUCTION

Surrealism is important not only as a historical movement but also as an attempt to redefine the world, to reveal "the real function of the mind" (Surrealist Manifesto, 1924) following almost exactly Freud's distinction between reflective thinking and auto-observation of freewheeling thoughts. In this way the analytic method of automatic thinking developed, as also those experiments in automatic writing whose seriousness has often been contested, or misconstrued as just another "Baroque" manner of literary composition. Who can deny today that our way of thinking, feeling and existing has been profoundly altered by the Surrealist Manifestos? Yet there are many who go on, as Heraclitus would put it, as if "they had a wisdom of their own."

The early part of Andreas Embiricos' collection of texts is poems in prose, in the tradition of Baudelaire, Rimbaud, Nerval, Breton and Eluard. They are the fruit of a "lyrical" experience — enriched by the "experience" of psychoanalysis — for Embiricos is not only the first Greek surrealist poet, but also the first Greek psychoanalyst. His images range from "symbolic figures" like the sleepwalking girl who never wakes up and who becomes more and more beautiful every year, to descriptions of landscapes, reminding one of Bertrand's *Gaspard de la Nuit*, in which the observer is incorporated in the end himself. He uses parables of sex-awakening and spring, awakenings of the life-force that recall D. H. Lawrence, dreamlike incestuous tendencies, in which the utterances of names like Dioscuros and Amalia take on the significance of "keys" to undisclosed realities. What a pity my name is Amalia, exclaims a girl, in love with her brother, voicing her regret of the taboo; such surprise effects are not alien to Embiricos. Voices whispering mysterious names that evoke a mythical context, Merope, Nausica, Ariadne, Alkmene, Corinna, abound in these texts, or are reduced to exclamations like the "Ea, Ea" of Creole women. Small boys are named by some Alasvir (an imaginary name), by others "small but sure cherries" — becoming elements of Nature. The technique of automatism, used by Embiricos, centers on themes of "recognition," of affinities, visions, words, notions like sudden illuminations. In the second and third sections the prose poems develop into something more rare: into a kind of "tale" whose latent or even obvious content has a definite meaning, illustrative of a philosophy of life.

The mysterious function of desire through dreams and transpositions or transformations of the objects of desire are poetically realized in a story called *Madalenia*. The narrator, dropping asleep under a tree, finds himself, after a sensation of falling, on his native island of Andros (also Embiricos' island). Wandering in the countryside he hopes to come on some country girl to make love to. He notices a large 1,000-ton clipper close to the shore. He feels mysteriously attracted to the boat, as if to a woman. Noises of love-making like those in adjoining rooms of hotels or houses are heard. Venus, the planet, shines in the heavens. Nothing stirs on board. In his haste, the narrator jumps on a slumbering boat in the harbor and rows out to the clipper. Above the prow of the boat he distinguishes a sculpted mermaid or gorgon. To his amazement, she is alive, she breathes. He calls her Venus (Aphrodite) but she answers "No, my name is Madalenia." The ship is a desired woman mythically realized by the dreamer. So far so good: but how does one explain that reality also conspires in the game of the subconscious world—and the two become one? For the narrator, awakening, comes upon a statue (a copy of the Venus de Milo in a neighboring garden) upon whose base some hand has scribbled the name "Madalenia." The meaning of the story (the clipper has a crew of dwarfs dressed up as seventeenth-century pirates behaving rather like those in Rip van Winkle) is nevertheless close to the psychoanalytical meaning that Freud drew from Jensen's story *Gradiva*, in which a young visitor to Pompeii sees an apparition and falls madly in love with her, only to discover she was his neighbor, a girl he had known, perhaps loved, when he was a boy, but whom he had "forgotten." Thus the copy of the Venus de Milo — "forgotten" by the narrator — is transformed and cosmically interpreted in his dream.

The theme of recognition, which is also self-recognition, frequently occurs in the later stories. Embiricos is unique in that he is an authentic poet and at the same time a professional psychoanalyst. His characters, defying convention, customs, inhibition, shame or other prejudices, often behave like the ancient Gods, in their murderous or pleasure-seeking expeditions, fulfilling instincts that are latent in every human being. For Embiricos the important thing is self-realization — whether in man, woman or child — the manifestation, often in a magical manner, of the inner self, condemned by guilt to "the dungeons of the Ego." But Embiricos' importance (over and above his qualities as a stylist where he approaches Kalvos, Kavafis and Papadiamantis, in his ingenious combination of colloquial, vernacular or "demotic" Greek, with the formal "purist" language) is not confined to his psychoanalytical discoveries. He also attacks the problem of self, of identities: who are we? Why are we? In a short narrative poem called *Nerone*, the narrator, describing a scene in the Roman arena, finally realizes that he himself is the Emperor. Hermolaos the Macedonian is magically connected, according to his description, to an event that was due to happen sixteen years later: in this instance the narrator, on a visit to Delphi, has a clairvoyant vision of the future birth of Alexander the Great.

In the poem called the *Texts* (also meaning in Greek what lies low), the fate of a besieged city is intimately connected with the existence of an unknown cyclist. This relates perhaps to one of the first psychoanalytical interpretations of dreams known to us: by the soothsayer Aristandros to the dream of Alexander the Great when he was vainly besieging the city of Tyre. Alexander dreamt of Satyros (one of the well-known followers of the Greek god Pan) but Satyros in Greek could also mean "yours is Tyre"; upon which Alexander, encouraged, conquers the city. (Freud, *The Interpretation of Dreams.)* In another story, the identity of an unknown benefactor of the city of Lionville who transforms a drab city into a paradise is unexpectedly revealed by Chance (Tyche), a young girl who sells postcards and with whom the inquirer-narrator has a love affair. By kissing the postcard representing the hero she has given him, the narrator's lips tear off the covering cape and the benefactor is revealed as...But I will let the reader guess. This story has a certain affinity to the "magical" or "initiatory" tales of antiquity, to *The Golden Ass* of Apuleius, for example, or the *Life of Apollonios of Tyana*. All Embiricos' work has this double character. Another story — perhaps the most impressive — is called *Neoptolemos the First, King of the Greeks (Pages from a Diary)*. In this a case of megalomaniac delirium is described. The narrator is a patient recently released from a lunatic asylum, considered as cured by the authorities. He is particularly grateful to a poet-psychoanalyst, to whose understanding he owes his cure. For he is well now, a greater genius than before, the son of Achilles, he is 3,000 years old, he is now a man. His decision is taken! He is going to claim the throne of Greece, and his first act (he is taking the bus to Delphi on that very day) will be to blow up the sanctuary of Apollo who was "responsible for the death of his father." In this story Embiricos' fulfilment and realization of "desire" takes on the form of lunacy. His secret sympathy with the "lunatic" shows that Embiricos is not a doctor, but a poet. No ordinary psychiatrist would ever have written like this: for the lunatic's only crime was to destroy the "Statue of Logic" — the initial reason for his internment.

Again, the ruses and artifices of desire are wonderfully described in the story *The Maid of Pennsylvania*, where a young man succeeds in having a love affair with a girl of twelve by disguising himself as a governess. This transvestite of unusual kind confesses his deception, as did the hero of *Lolita*, but the reader, seduced by the writing as much as by the story, remains involved, exactly as the ancient spectator of a Greek tragedy, knowing by heart what he was going to see, still looked forward to it with renewed excitement.

Embiricos, in this book, touches us in unique fashion by combining history and myth, poetry and psychology, to create a generous and splendid universe in which erotic passion has free play and the ordinary is transformed by poetic imagination into something extraordinary. Not something which is only "technical" or "formal," or just "beautiful," but also tremendously important, one feels, for the future of humanity.

— NANOS VALAORITIS

INSTEAD OF A PROLOGUE

AMOUR AMOUR

To Vivika

Once, many years ago, while on an excursion in Switzerland, I stopped to admire a huge waterfall which pounded over granite rocks among rich vegetation. During that period, which I could call a period of intense research, forced by an inner necessity that was almost organic, I was trying to find a more immediate and a fuller expression in the poems which I then wrote. The sight of the waterfall suddenly gave me an idea. As I saw the water falling from high up to continue on its gurgling way, I thought how interesting it would be if I could use, in the spheres of poetic creation, the same process which makes the flowing of the falling water such a rich, fascinating and indisputable reality, instead of describing this flowing or some other phenomenon, event, feeling or idea on the basis of a preconceived and predetermined plan or formula.

I wanted, in other words, to weave in my poems all those elements which, whether we want this or not, are precluded from or evade us, in traditional poetry. I wanted to include in my poems those elements in such a way that a poem would not merely consist of one or more subjective or objective themes, logically specified and developed within conscious limits, but of any elements which would appear in the flux of its becoming regardless of any conventional or standardized aesthetic, ethical or logical construction. In this case, I thought, we would have a dynamic and total poem, a self-subsistent poem, a poem-event in place of consecutive presentations of static descriptions of certain events or sentiments, in this or that technique.

From the day this idea came to me, I wished to apply it and so I started writing new poems attempting to achieve what I was after. These poems, showed, naturally, great development and a marked difference from previous ones, but these too, although I liked them more than those I wrote before, did not satisfy me in my quest. Although they differed from the previous ones in form, they did not differ enough in essence. It was clear to me that what was missing was the appropriate means that would serve to realize the objective aim. I thought, however, that the only way I could meet all those difficulties would be not by resigning but by continuing my explorations and so I continued writing with the certainty that my original idea was a good one and that sooner or later I would find the way to make it bear me fruit. Who knows, maybe I would still be searching today if what was for me a shattering confrontation with surrealism had not opened my eyes. From that day on, I can say that almost at once I made out where the road lay and I threw myself with enthusiasm and true exaltation in the stream of this historic movement. I had heard its calling and I followed it. I had heard its voice, that voice which, as André Breton said so rightly in his first manifesto, continues chanting even on the eve of death and over storms.

In what I have said before, I do not mean to imply that my personal pre-surrealist theories were identical with, or similar to the context of surrealism, nor am I going to pose here as its predecessor. These theories have, of course, a relationship with the surrealist ones. But, in general, surrealism goes beyond my original objectives and, what is more, provides the means for the practical application of its content opening up horizons even wider than those I saw in my personal beliefs. I once more take this opportunity to express here my admiration and gratitude for André Breton and the other surrealists who, after Sigmund Freud and the psychoanalysts, have shed, in our age, the most illuminating light on the thick darkness that surrounds us.

And so a new world opened up before me, like a sudden bursting into bloom of inexhaustible miracles, a world around me and in me that was unending and immeasurable, a truly magic world to which surrealism has given us once and for all the right keys.

Look how one sentence becomes a corvette sailing away in fair wind like a cloud blown by a sea wind or the north wind. A reflection sounds, a drop floods and a voice blossoms. A child stands erect in the clearing of a silent forest and suddenly grows before a woman. A dress becomes a brilliant aurora borealis. A photograph lives with an action of its own which is interwoven with the life of the spectator like a coin, a crystal or a glove. Behold a newspaper that is transformed into a sweet-smelling forest or a plateau with snow-covered cordilleras. Poetry is transfused into life and life into poetry. Our participation in any phenomenon or event is no longer impossible. A sentiment, an urge, a word, they may all become concrete beings, glittering objects with throbbing life, having their own form.

Having made this discovery and with my consequent accession to the surrealist movement, I put aside not only my old techniques, but also every sort of pride in myself and self-boasting of the kind one so often finds among poets and artists who can accept nothing else in the world outside themselves and no other contribution to poetry and life except for what results out of their narrow selfishness and inconceivable narcissism.

Here I must add that two things helped me considerably to a quick understanding and assimilation of surrealism: my psychoanalytic knowledge and the philosophy of Hegel. From that day on, I started using the technique of automatic writing. I wrote poetry and prose feverishly and with the true passion of the novice. Later (in 1935) I collected a few of my surrealist writings and had them published under the title *Blast Furnace*. This book constitutes the first genuine manifestation and the first act of surrealism in Greece, with the exception of a lecture which I gave on this movement and its objectives during the spring of the same year.

Many critics at that time spoke and wrote derisively of that book and of the movement which it represented. Today some of them flirt with the surrealists, speaking of a "well-meant" surrealism — (what can this be?) — on which they now ridiculously want to pass judgment while some time ago they had been spreading the rumor that surrealism had been dead and buried. Of course, they maintain many reservations, typical of their lack of courage, concerning what constitutes precisely the backbone and the essence of the theory, and thus they prove — at least most of them — that either they have understood nothing at all or that they are desperately trying to restore their shaken authority before the eyes of the public and the young poets whose interest in surrealism increases from day to day. *

I see, however, that this topic is leading me elsewhere and I hasten to return to what interests me.

I can say, then, that the waterfall of which I spoke at the beginning did not stop in Switzerland. Its water falls from a great height, rolls down and continues to flow. Inside and on the spume of the consecutive falls, I can see large and transparent spheres, as if made of crystal, in the hands of foam-covered dancers. I can see them jumping and col-

---

* *Amour Amour* was written in 1939.

liding with each other, sometimes carried away by the force of the water and sometimes sliding away to rise like balloons that slip out of the hands of ecstatic children in gardens or squares. I see them caught up in the water again, dancing again on the milk-white foam which delights in its flow while sprinkling the observer and the branches around with the dew of the foamy powder it scatters, like a cloud that brings a drizzle, in the thunderous downpour of the waterfall.

The glory of this cataract is the glory of Rio Bogota. Its magic is the magic of the triple cascade of the valley of Hyossemita. Its charm is the charm of all the waterfalls of the Alps, the Pyrenees and the Apennines. Its sound is the voice of an angel falling for ever and ever in a chaotic abyss. His shattered wings are mixed up, interwoven with the spume of the fall and an eagle balances high up on the air listening to the never-ending song of the sound thundering for ever, and as if uttering "ahaaha," like an echo bouncing back from caves and abysmal depths.

The water continues to flow from height to depth, rolling its thunder, and as it falls it forms in front of the black granite an uninterrupted ladder of spray that disappears in the azure of the sky above.

The cataract delights in its metamorphosis and transforms itself from heavy downpour to an unobstructed current which flows first in the bed of a narrow torrent and then winds out in the ravine and beyond the valley in a fast current which irrigates thick river banks and, as it gets wider, it becomes calmer, silently concealing its strength in its open stretch — just the same as the one which spreads back, now, to the years of my childhood when I, too, got to know the Danube and the wide rivers.

O, the beautiful Baragan! Braila, Ismaili and Picket! The perfumed plains of Valachia at harvest time! The haystacks raised like golden castles surrounded by a sea of wheat, the sickles shining with such impetus and strength that, if it were not day but night, they would mow down even the stars. The machines thresh and sift the wheat, and fluid time flows and goes but is never lost; on the contrary, it lives on, accumulating in visions and in reminiscences. A woman hastily stops working to give birth to a child in a ditch. The train crosses the plain. A bird flies away frightened. A stallion rides a mare. Around them gypsy boys and girls shout for joy and their voices vibrate together with the chirping of the crickets that flood the air. The light is warm and the valley is steaming in the sun. In the shade of a haystack, a young blonde girl, bare breasted, her blouse open because of the heat, is tired of reading the adventures of Potemkin in Bessarabia and puts the book aside. But before even she has finished doing so, her gaze rests on the lovemaking of the horses and the nearby children imitating them. The stallion standing on his hind legs dominates the mare. In a little while he is on his fours again and the children scatter and leave. The young girl shuts her eyes and sees before her Potemkin. No need even to talk to him. Potemkin turns around and takes her from the waist. She receives him as the mare has received the stallion and the sighs that escape her lips are so ardent that the crickets stop chirping.

That is how the wheat is poured into the storehouses. That is how visions and reminiscences accumulate. All kinds of boats move on the river. They belong to so many nations that what I have best stored in my memory is the colors rather than the shapes of the flags of each. Wheat silos and oil-pipes never stop in cities like Galatzi and Constanza. A multitude of boats come and go. I stand on the deck of one of these and leaning on the rail I look at the Danube and its vast horizons, dazzled again as when I was a child and saw the river for the first time and its beloved, unencumbered plains.

This boat transports me to Russia as I knew it in my childhood when I traveled there with my mother who came from there. Events from that period, as also many other events from other periods in my life (some of which have great importance for me because of their effect and repercussions), appear to me like clear pictures, neither immobile, nor completely isolated from each other, as, for example, a series of photographs arranged chronologically would appear in an album. These pictures move; they communicate with each other, they cluster together; they have a *modus vivendi* and a *status quo* of their own; none of them is absolutely confined in strictly specified frames; their relationships are not defined by a conscious mechanism; they have an autonomy the structure of which is not regulated by the will but by an automatic and unconscious propelling energy which escapes the control of the conscious side of personality, as happens during the moments just before being completely awake or in the intoxication of sleep, or, even better, as happens in dreams. An image may very well coexist with another; it can be imprinted or superimposed upon another that precedes or follows without obliterating it, or it can receive on its surface a new image without itself disappearing, as happens in the printing of photographs or in movie pictures.

These images may, of course, have a logical or illogical association which, in a way, becomes the subject. But it is possible for another correlative association to steal in on this subject which may, at first, seem to be an unrelated or parasitic element, while it is actually related. This may result in an amalgam of two or more images which will constitute a new image, similar to what we would get if, in the scene of a theatrical play a character of another play walked in, or some other person, to take an organic part in the development of the action; as, for example, Othello in the scene of the assassination of Caesar, or I in the balcony scene of Romeo and Juliet. This does not often happen in poetry or art which are under the control of logic.

It happens, however, continuously in our feelings, our dreams and our imaginings. And this will always happen not to the detriment, as many think, but to the greatly enriching benefit of poetry and art, whenever a poet or an artist accepts to use what, in essence, constitutes becoming itself, and the very substance not only of poetry but of life itself.

The boat that transports me to Russia anchors at Sebastopol. After staying for a few days in this beautiful city of the Crimea, I go to visit the estates which belonged to my uncles before the 1917 Revolution. Tsorgun, a village half inhabited by Tartars and the other half by Russians, is mixed in my memory with a multitude of reminiscences from my childhood. Even today, when I hear horses galloping on a wooden bridge or the sound of iron carriage wheels, I can see before me the old wooden bridge, over the small river Tsornayia near the house of my uncle Dimitri who, with love and infinite kindness, had always offered me his hospitality whenever I went to visit his estates as a child.

From the top of a big bushy oak tree, on the bank of Tsornayia, or having climbed up the branches of a plum tree so loaded with plums that a strong shake would bring them down in a shower, I often saw the Tartar boys walking nude in the river near the wooden bridge where the water was deeper. There they bathed together, shouting while their horses splashed around them. Their words had the exciting, explicit, inarticulate quality of sounds which spring up like darting sperm from the instincts and the entrails of human beings.

The boys' games were mainly of two kinds, warlike and erotic. A boy would mercilessly drench a younger boy. Another boy tried to hit a dog with stones. A third boy would suddenly straddle one of the horses and ride into the river pushing the others aside, shouting triumphantly and adding to this epic action a paean of gargling laughter and sharp curses. And while some boys wrestled on the soft ground near the river, others, standing on the river bank, competed with each other in who could piss furthest. Others, still, whipped up erections and keenly compared their penises. Of these, some tossed themselves or each other off, while others, more aloof, withdrew to quiet and deserted parts of the river bank where they silently masturbated, emitting moans and sighs behind the branches of trees or thick bushes. The more courageous and slightly more mature boys proceeded to another part of the river, not very far from the wooden bridge, where the water was shallower and where young Tartar girls with tufted loose trousers, and half-nude gypsy girls often came to water their horses. For some of these that was the furthest point of their advances, though they did not want to lose face by seeming to return unappeased. They tended to settle on a symbolic middle course, confining themselves to arrogant exhibitions of their penises and from a safe distance sprinkling the grass and the river with milky spurts. The more daring aggressive ones dashed unblushingly forward trying to push up against the bare bodies of the girls whose dresses allowed an occasional glimpse of pubic hair and vagina. The young Tartar and gypsy girls remained rooted to the spot, though not without observing the genitals of the boys with a mixture of wishful interest and frightened curiosity. But when some of these made to jump on them, they would run away like frightened pigeons or start screaming for help from parents or passers-by who would disperse the young conquerors with shouts, stones and curses. Group seduction was no help to any of them. Results were only possible when a boy went out hunting without his comrades and happened to come upon a young girl alone. Sometimes then the young boy, especially if the girl was acquiescent, managed to do everything.

Besides these concrete recollections, many other similar but vaguer ones slowly converge on Tsorgun, tending to transform the small river Tsornayia to a large one running not through the Crimea, but through a continent which has been arbitrarily created by me and the boundaries of which become indefinite and finally disappear, lost in the dominion of my subjective "hinterland" in a manner similar to the complicated mechanism which we discover in dreams and illusions.

The exploits of the young Tartars and their erotic adventures concentrate, in my mind, on the banks of the river Amour. The fact that the name of this river means "love," in French, and the fact that Amour flows through countries inhabited by Mongol races, to which the Tartars of my childhood reminiscences also belong, have made me choose this river in Siberia. But my love for this distant land, which symbolizes to me other archetypes of love — Russia, mother — (my mother is half Russian) — has also played an important role in its choice. Since the moment of its discovery, it has constituted a point of take-off and return for the multitude of correlations which come and leave my mind in waves like ebb and tide.

And the river Amour always irrigates this country. The epic of the young Tartars of Tsorgun is followed here, like an echo of their shouts, by the war cries of the Mongols and the Kozacks and the other fighting riders beyond the steppes of the Kirghiz. The vast deserted expanses which are covered in parts by tundra, in the flame of summer, and in other parts by huge thick forests, are traversed by the small sinewy horses of the nomads and the conquerors while sleepless eagles and vultures, always ready to attack, travel in the azure air over the Altai and the Yablonei mountains pillaging on their way the fauna of the high plateaus. Suddenly a shrill cry rips the air. This time it does not come from an animal that has been ripped by the claws and the beak of a vulture. A puff of smoke bursts on the horizon and it is immediately followed by many others, so many that they form a cloud blown in the direction of the wind. A thumping subterranean thunder grows louder and nearer as if a herd of mammoths or gigantic stags of the

Quaternary was passing. The Trans-Siberian, the steel king of Asia, goes by.

And Amour continues its flow, irrigating not only the countries which it traverses from the Yablonei mountains to its mouth in the Sea of Okhotsk, but also the whole of my hinterland into which it has penetrated and of which only a small part is contained in these pages.

Thus, to me, Amour the river is always Amour-Love.

Towards it, will always converge, and from it will always spring forth all our wishes and impulses, whether consciously or unconsciously. On its banks, we shall wage war and make peace, we shall destroy and create, we shall toil and repose, we shall lament and exult, we shall thirst and quench thirst, those of us who say "yes" and those of us who say "no."

I said always. Yes. Always and ever, Amour will flow, both inside and outside, in its all-ruling might, like yesterday, like today, as it floods now inside me and overflows, forcing me to shout with all the power of my lungs:

"Amour! Amour!"

THE DOVE-COT

1

She had adorned her table with the bridal veils of three young girls, one of whom had remained a virgin. As soon as she had finished, she took off her silk stockings and sat down. She was waiting for the carriage that would bring her the horses. But, suddenly, her brother broke into the room bellowing out: "Dioscuros! Pity on others and on ourselves!" Like a good sister, the young girl returned to the table and breaking the necklace which was around her neck, sprinkled the carpet, the furniture and the bridal veils with the amber berries. She then took her breasts out of her blouse and lay on the table.

2

The young man, full of remorse, opened the door again and approached his sleeping sister on tip-toe. He wore a helmet on his head but for the rest he was partially naked. From the waist down he wore his mother's dress, and sandals on his feet. When he had made certain that the young girl was asleep, he opened the window to ensure the mob understood that they should keep silent.

3

All the things told him by his sister at different times fell on the carpet now. Some looked like anemones, others like partridge and others still like amazones. The young man was unable to hold back his tears. The phrase which he had uttered a little while ago seemed to him cruel and unfeeling, and unwillingly he compared it with the exquisite breasts of his sister.

4

He was no hero. (His feeling; it reminded him of falls of apples.)

5

He was inhuman. (He felt the world his own, but very bitter.)

6

He was a hero but inhuman — like a man that

crushes a medusa under his foot.

7

His sobs began to choke him. Deeply conscious of the weight of that phrase, he bent and kissed his sister's two breasts. Then he went out and, closing the door hastily behind him, mingled with the crowd.

8

The young girl awoke with the double kiss. Besides, she was not really asleep; she was only pretending. Even her silence expressed her emotion. As soon as the door had closed, she stood up in distress and approached the window. Both her brother and the crowd had vanished and the emptiness of the road resembled the lavish morning sunlight. The young girl ripped her blouse and her breasts and cried with all the strength of her soul: "What a pity that my name is Amalia!"

She closed the window.

SITE

To Matsi

You were like a silence penetrated by the **wind**.
However, I had healed your wound and the words
we spoke had come so close to us that both silence
and the vacuum of the days before we met, completely disappeared. The site where we met, which
has become the site of our love, does not conform
to its neighbors. You are good and your beauty ex-
ceeds the boundaries of the city and reaches the
outskirts of your past loneliness, which you yourself
have abolished. Yes, there are no others in this site.
I am near you and I inhabit your hopes as you inhabit my eyelids when I sleep. The words of others
have no meaning because they lost the character
they had before we met and their faces have begun
to resemble the faces of strangers unknown to me
and perhaps even to you. What does it matter,
though? The shell of the past has broken and you
came out of it, full, definite, in velvet, leaving your
breasts half bare. That is why I will never forget
this site. I shall buy it and never sell it. That is why
I tell you that I am like a stone which you hold in

your hand; a warm stone which throbs with every heartbeat in the sensuousness of your touch. When recollections of bygone years awake in it, they will seem to us both like fossil chronicles of history, because stones too have their history like the stone which you will hold in your hand. That is why I shall not sell this site but shall keep it with all its stones, with all its jewels, with all its ornaments, and let the others search for what they want in their own foundations.

The machines and the sickles of our land have not yet been bought. But this, my love, does not mean that our wheat will not be threshed. It will be threshed some day and those who pick the crop will be us again, one thousand times us, our hands stretched out over our valleys and over the valleys of our children. A child may search bending among the wheat, to find a button or a glittering May-bug, but this does not mean that our wheat will remain unthreshed. There is nothing more graceful than the steps of growing children. There is nothing more predictable than the steps of grown-ups. There is nothing more beautiful than the raised eyes and arms of people who, taking their clothes off, get ready to release the desires of their bodies. Even their most insignificant movements may bear fruit; they may become workshops with beds of flowers in the fury of the fields. My love, I said workshops. These workshops will be ours; bright institutions, rosy and erect and buzzing whenever we pass their thresholds, interpreters of their activities or like threshers of the surrounding wheat, the wheat that spurts from the earth the way involuntary cries spurt from the mouths of women in orgasm.

My love, I love you and our journey will be like a procession of perfumes in the spring.

THE RIBBON

To Maria Kozadinou

The street was empty, emptier than an empty drawer, and it unwound like the white ribbon which the young daughter of the house had stolen a few days ago from her mother, taking it out of a drawer in her toilet table. Shut in her own room, the young girl had tried the ribbon on again and again, this way and that way, on her hair, round her neck and on her breasts while looking at herself in the mirror. The white contrast of the ribbon on the black dress fascinated her so much that whenever she had a free moment she rushed to her bedroom and tried it on again, dreaming of beautiful hats, azure, yellow and green dresses stamped with many-colored branches and flowers or with fascinating small designs repeated at intervals not only on the cloth, but also on her body — which she also dreamed of being larger, with fuller breasts, more prominent hips, like her mother's.

This poetic but finally obsessive mood lasted for about a week, until, in fact, it was eclipsed by the violent feeling of hatred which overcame her mother when she discovered the theft. Unmoved by the innocent attempts of her daughter to excuse herself, she dismissed her, having first thrashed her while screaming at the top of her voice so raucously that all the members of the family were afraid it might break. The voice, nevertheless, did not break. A crack, however, appeared on the wall of the house and through this the young girl ran away, following the street which unwound before her like the ribbon which she still held in her left hand. The girl in her terror ran as fast as she could, the street being empty. Time sped by. It must have been midday, but she still could not stop, though exhausted. Once only she paused, thunderstruck. She had heard a voice ripping the air density of thin glass: "Merope! Merope!" But there was no one there, so she continued running at the same speed. Perhaps she would have gone still further if she had not come to thorny fields, fields full of stones that tore the soft soles of her feet. Unable to continue, and in great distress, a course that was cruel, unjust, with no paved street or benches, she was finally forced to stop. She felt like a heavy drop hanging on the brink, ready to fall. A sob rose from her chest to her throat, but had no time to burst from her. Her ears were already buzzing as she fell to the stony ground as if struck by thunder. Then sleep, sudden and deep, overtook her.

Now she was moving on the shore of her lethargy, briskly and without meeting any obstacles, in the way half-nude morning breezes move, in the spring, over the lightly waving sea. Repeated gusts made the folds of her dress flap and her falling hair waved like a mane. A caressing and open-sea whisper echoed in her ears a vague name, as if heard indirectly, from a great distance repeating: "Nausica! Nausica!" Writhing sea-stars and crosses mingled with the sleeping girl's steps and she crushed them with the soles of her feet. The powder-thin sand softened the wounds of her feet and every one of her steps remained so deeply imprinted that the prints can still be clearly seen. A man, red like a red Indian healer-priest, sitting on the sand, suddenly stopped the young girl, and with quenching solicitousness enough to satisfy the thirst of a land like the *Terra del Fuego*, laid her down and treated her burning, bleeding feet. He took the ribbon which she held in her hand, cut it in two pieces of equal size and tied each band round her ankles like leather straps. Ever since, the young girl continually wanders along the shore, walking as if awake, although she is asleep, from one end to the other. She becomes more and more beautiful every year and, in spite of the efforts of curious tourists who come to see her from all parts of the world, no one has ever succeeded in waking her.

THE TEXTS

To Nikos Gatsos

Behind the walls.

In the anxiety of a beleaguered city.

In the houses, mistresses and maids, after the curfew, sparingly fed the fires with the last stored chopped wood, adding old shelves, boxes, all sorts of rubbish and even frames of paintings. Groceries, markets and bakeries were all completely closed down, their place taken by a few state distributors guarded by army detachments with machine guns. The little food available was given to the hungry population on ration books and in very small quantities. With the exception of a few military vehicles and still fewer trams, there circulated in the streets only some buses, a few emaciated pedestrians and one cyclist.

This man was middle-aged and wore ordinary civilian clothes. Although completely unknown before the siege he became well known to all by the end of the first month. Although the sight of him frightened the inhabitants, although he did not become popular even for a moment, he succeeded, in spite of this, in becoming necessary not only to the eyes of the people but to the conscience of the authorities as well. All considered him in some way or another as the animator of the hopeless defense.

Sitting on his saddle, he went coolly round the city cycling day and night, even during the heaviest moments of bombardment. Nobody knew where he came from. Nobody knew who he was. Nobody could boast that he had pushed aside even one fold of the mystery that surrounded and followed him everywhere. He alone seemed to know everything. Casually making his way into all quarters of the city (much as the hand of a skilful pickpocket slips into the purse) he frightened the inhabitants. At the same time he inspired them with new strength, giving them faith in the happy outcome of the war. This he did, not with words, but through his modest, unconcerned expression, the steady revolution of his bicycle-chain, the powerful repetitiveness of his innumerable passings. There was no exhibitionism, no acrobatic showings off or rabble rousing, nothing of this kind to account for the extraordinary and deep impression he produced on the inhabitants.

Once, on the first day of his rounds, which later became legendary, a greengrocer slung a basket at his head. At the same second the largest credit establishment in the city crashed to the ground. A few days later, an old woman attempted to stab him with her umbrella. The same moment, a fire broke out in the cathedral and burned it down.

Since then, no one ever thought of attacking the cyclist or preventing his passing. The truth is that he was never loved by the inhabitants. But while they all considered him an evil omen at first, little by little, and without anyone knowing the reason why, each one of them, without exception, began to think of him as a symbol of victory and therefore as good luck. During the last week the population completely identified its destiny with the destiny of the cyclist. Some offered him flowers, others a little food and others still tubes or other accessories for his decrepit bicycle. He, however, refused to accept anything and continued on his way day and night, resting for about two hours each day on a bench in a quiet corner of the public garden.

During the third month of the siege, however, this man expressed a wish that was in the nature of a demand. The mayor had invited him one morning to offer him, on behalf of the inhabitants, a new bicycle. The cyclist did not accept the present but asked to receive the young and beautiful wife of the mayor in marriage.

The mayor, insulted, hit the man. The cyclist fell and in falling was seriously wounded. After a while, the city was informed that, in spite of the doctors' treatment, he was at the hospital and dying.

That same day the mayor was assassinated. The inhabitants, terrified, prayed in their houses, in the churches, and in front of the hospital, begging that the dying man be saved.

But there seemed no hope. On the contrary, heavy clouds gathered over the city and on the evening of the same day, the enemy, breaking through the walls, entered the suburbs and advanced into the main squares.

On the following day, the cyclist died. Few escaped. The men were slaughtered, the women and the children were taken slaves, the city was burned, and on its ruins the conquerors established the bicycle-racing stadium where the greatest and most glorious bicycle races take place today.

LAND OF LANDSCAPE

To Matsi

At a certain point, dominated on the right by a massive steep rock and on the left by a smaller and milder rocky projection, a space opens up beyond which a slope stretches gently away in a series of harmonious folds of the ground. It is a gradual affair, a kind of declivity many parts of which are grassy while others are bare, reappearing covered with grass and thick shrubs or small bushy trees.

The soil is, in some places, thick and reddish in the bare parts, while in others, it is thinner, grainy and a sort of ochre. The folds vary in color, as well as in formation and shape. Thus, while some hillocks point like firm breasts, others have the protuberance of a pulsating pubic mound; the slopes and the ascents, as well as the alternations of grassy and bare expanse, combine to give a fluid grace to the landscape, due, on the one hand, to the formation of the ground and, on the other, to the changes from grassy to dry texture, as well as to variation in the intensity of the colors. This sensation is so acute that it provides the illusion of a double view, of both an uninterrupted and concrete view of the landscape and the fleeting vague image of a dancer the hem of whose wide and deeply-folded dress rocks rhythmically in a whirling dance; or the illusion may be of waves that do not break but are only smooth curved swellings and alternating foamless hollows where the liquid element has become concrete matter, like many-colored sections of the sea crystallized calm after a violent storm. The impression which this part of the landscape gives is an impression of tranquillity, a calm which has followed a tempest, or a violent and beneficial storm, the most basic and vital elements of which have not disappeared but continue existing in a way that makes calmness a vigorous and throbbing serenity, like that of lovers who in the interval between two bouts of love-making — satisfied desire stirring into ripening lust — experience the simultaneous glow of both appeasement and want.

The serenity which bathes the entire landscape applies exactly to the serenity of this simile; and it is so clear that it reverberates like the clear sound of a bell, the bottomless depth of which seems increased by the two or three light clouds floating on the horizon.

Another element which is an important factor in the landscape is the tree which rises up, not far off, just below the rocky projection on the left, on the edge of the slight slope. This tree is so large, and its foliage so thick, that one could mistake it at first sight for a whole cluster of trees. One of the lower branches droops downwards, its hanging leaves dipping lightly in a stream which after disappearing from sight behind one of the bare folds in the ground reappears winding calmly in the middle of green meadows.

Abundant light shines upon the tufts of the foliage but only with difficulty manages to penetrate its inner thickness, making the shade under the leafy surface in consequence so deep it has a different color. The antagonism between light and dark green is so intense that one not only sees the separation of the colors but may also feel, at the same time, the warmth of the sun and the coolness of the shade. And while on the outer surface of the tree the light chants and occasionally bubbles out in erotic exaltation, the shade coils in the depths of the foliage, a silent collector of secrets and confidences.

Observe how looking at the outer surface of the

foliage is identical to our participation in the raising of a flag, to the explosion of a cry of joy or to the sudden shooting out from deep within of a powerful spring, whenever the sun plays on the leaves and spreads abundant iridescent light. Observe how staring into the shade of the inner, velvet thickness of the foliage is akin to climbing down a cave full of stalactites, entering the labyrinth of an anguished confession, or a cathedral resounding with the rustling of prayers and sighs of sad people.

In this ambiguous atmosphere, which emanates from the tree and also surrounds it, a young woman might well be setting out, heedlessly and in free acceptance of her feelings, to meet her ardent suitor, or an adulteress, full of anxiety and with a thousand precautions, going in fear and guilt to meet her hesitating lover.

In the places around this landscape, which does not seem at all to be near the Equator, or in a torrid zone, the vegetation still seems vaguely tropical. An explorer could easily come upon a herd of antelope who, upon hearing someone cough or a sudden creaking from a dried branch on which someone has stepped, breaking it, would start gracefully away, fear, of which these slender animals are always captive, lending them its own especial beauty. And this explorer, soothed by the feelings which his participation in this landscape had aroused in him, might perfectly well write or recite the poem which I include in this text, as an inseparable part of the landscape:

"The forest shudders in the bindweed of the snakes that constrict it, and the Equator warms the cracks of an improvised hut. A creole is sunbathing on the roof and she gradually turns into a white woman wanting to tan. On the other side of the Equator, two women and two men are shouting: 'Ea! Ea!' and the frightened antelope run and hurl themselves down the precipices roaring in anticipation of receiving them. This is how the antelope were slaughtered. Their entrails vibrate in the mouths of the precipices. But the men and women, still seeing on the horizon the outline of the fear and the flight of the tender herd, and in spite of the sorrow they have felt, continue shouting: 'Ea! Ea!' because the day is beautiful and blissful, full of butterflies. Two or three puffs of white and extremely light cloud are formed in the blue sky from the sighs which the happy creole utters."

WINDOW LIGHT

To George Gounaropoulos

The light came through the open window and bathed the face and figure of the girl who was looking out. Spring triumphed and, with every moment, its dominating presence was made more and more felt in a way, violent as well as constant, that already announced the coming of summer. The pleasant warmth was so intense it made the flowers look as if they were changing from buds to blossoms instantaneously, as if this was a normal but exceptionally rapid function, something to be seen even by the naked eye.

The part played by the light was so important that the conventional outline of objects gave way under it, becoming faint or even disappearing, its place taken by forms dissolving and throbbing, substance changing into color, and continually defining, so to say, the participation of each object in nature by mutual and simultaneous interchange. Even shadows were brilliantly colored in the light and seemed non-existent where in fact they existed.

The light-colored dress of the girl gave the impression of spring, more and more apparent in the room where the diffused light now allowed a continual play of colors. The resemblance, or rather the identity of the atmosphere, between this and the other side of the open window transformed what was previously a closed space to a kind of annex to the open space outside, the light flooding the room being the same — throbbing, scented, full of competing and varied reflections on both sides of the window.

Thus, spring did not appear as a phenomenon recognizable only in nature but apparent wherever it was welcome, for example, in this room, the flowers of whose wallpaper had almost the fragrance of real flowers in a garden, and where, after pushing back the heavy curtains, the girl had opened the window and was looking outside. The colors of the room and of the objects which the room contained converged toward the girl, harmonising with her beautiful flesh in exactly the same way as her own colors merged, beyond the open window, with the foliage, the blossoms and the azure sky, in an identity of atmosphere and environment.

Bathed in this atmosphere, the girl stood by the

window looking out. Her dress, made of white transparent muslin, caressed almost her whole body. Her limbs trembled in consequence, like the colors in the light, and although they were covered by the dress, they were outlined behind its folds, especially her throbbing spherical breasts which looked, in their desire to free themselves even from this lightest of frothy coverings, as if they were about to burst out. The girl's hair, of a pale red tint, was really blonde and fell on her neck like a small waterfall, but held in place by a blue ribbon tied in a large bow on the front of her head. Her right arm rested on the window, looking like the neck of a swan pointing its beak in search of pickings in a pool or lake, while her left arm, hanging down as far as her thigh, ended in slender fingers lightly clasping an azure handkerchief ruffled as gently as her hair and skirt by the breeze which poured into the room like flowing clear water through a shining funnel. The almost bleeding lips of the girl were slightly parted and gave the impression that her breath would become visible at any moment — the incoming draft of air would suddenly appear like a rose-colored liquid when she inhaled, and when she breathed out a violent swarm of delicate feathers would emerge in a continuous flow of alternating matter and color.

The girl's expression and posture showed that she was completely at one with the season. Her eyes were blue, of a slightly deeper shade than the blue of the clear sky over the rustling trees beyond the window. They took on, as they gazed out over the shimmering foliage and sky, a musing quality, the throbbing transfiguration of the firmament passionately mirrored in their liquid depth.

And spring continued, under the girl's gaze, to spread and soar, its rich flow animating the girl's skin in analogous fashion and imparting to her a wondrous brilliance, her own color set off by the garden's flowers and fruit, around which buzzed gilded coleopters and other more delicate and transparent insects whose constant flutter was interrupted by the yellow and mauve of single or multicolored butterflies or by the sudden and quick darts of pursuing birds.

The feelings that consumed the girl at that moment were varied, and they fluttered back and forth, like her handkerchief, her skirt and her hair — even like she herself fluttered in the whirlwind of a dance, or whenever she rested on her back, after swimming, on the surface of a slightly rough sea.

What prevailed, however, and dominated, was a feeling equivalent to the quick melting of gold in the flames of a kiln, to a bubble bursting in a violent rush of wind, or to the dissolving of a clot which, becoming liquid, turns into a surging jet in the midst of the exclamations of hot-blooded men.

The young girl, still standing before the open window, continued to look out. Spring was completing its conquest and the light became warmer and warmer. From far away, behind the trees and bushes of the garden, from the depths of an age which was not exhausted by her memory, the same ancient, age-old and primary desire that she had known even in her very first youth, as a girl and as a child, invaded her, increasing the speed of her heart-beats so much that their repeated vibrations reached into her very womb.

"Yesterday" had then become "today" and "today" would soon become "tomorrow," that is, one more "today." And this would happen for ever, eternally, just as the colors of the kaleidoscope continually merge with each other and interlace, as an endless cochlea turns incessantly, interminably! O how azure the sky was, how clear, how high and immeasurable! What could this dazzling, unhesitating, irrevocable, brilliantly sparkling flood of light mean?

The girl's breath grew shorter. Her nostrils dilated and her breast heaved as if she would burst out in sobs. O, if only today would become "tomorrow" now. If only what would otherwise extend indefinitely the expectation in which she had always lived, could happen soon, before she petrified or turned into a stalactite. If only the edge could be taken off such sharp longing and anticipation. If only the utter, overbearing quiescence could suddenly be disturbed, the announcement come at last like the unexpected arrival of a white sailing boat.

But the girl could no longer breathe and her eyes, as she was looking at the sky, dilated, as if she was dazzled by the appearance of a fantastic crater. One minute, two minutes — behold, the bridegroom comes — and then she felt herself falling into an azure abyss, while somewhere in her consciousness bells tolled....Behold, the bridegroom comes....and the girl fell in a heap on the floor surrounded by the waves and the foam of her transparent dress.

At precisely the moment of her fainting, spring came to its incontrovertible climax, so that when, after a while, the girl recovered, summer, all-powerful, had arrived to glitter in the room as it did beyond the open window, as it did outside.

PUBERTY (The jewel)

It was in the days when ladies wore crinolines and men top hats, or, when traveling and on excursions, small, very small caps with a button in the middle.

Many of the passengers of the small steamship were sunbathing or strolling on the deck.

The day was beautiful. A light breeze fluttered the traveling veils of the ladies. A canary could be heard singing in a cabin. Three girls wearing large bows on their long wavy curls were playing on the deck, skipping.

Each jump they made was a small foamy aurora borealis. Their exclamations were the bursting into bloom of an azure or purple flower. Their every gaze was a glittering augury of summer's oncoming intensity.

Suddenly, a lady in a green dress said to her friend sitting beside her:

"My God, I forgot to put panties on my daughter....I must run and dress her immediately..."

Turning, then, to her daughter she cried:
"Yolanda....Yolanda....Come here."

Little Yolanda, bursting with happiness, was

still skipping. Her excitement was so intense it was impossible for her to hear her mother.

Several of the male passengers, sitting across from her, and pretending to be looking elsewhere, observed with quickening pulses that, under her lifted dress, her rosy and precocious love-flower was momentarily visible.

Yolanda's mother's friend turned to the anxious woman and interrupted her:

"Wait a minute, Elvira, let me finish what I was telling you about my sister-in-law....Besides, we city-people should breathe fresh air occasionally.... Let your daughter get some too. Let me finish what I was saying....Imagine, my sister-in-law told me that..."

The steamer was approaching port. Except for those observing Yolanda, all the others ran to the side of the boat where they could see the land.

"O, what a beautiful town!" some exclaimed.

"What a marvelous beach!...What beautiful lawns!" others said.

"A glorious day!...Such warmth and sun!" exclaimed another of Elvira's friends, addressing Yolanda's father who was standing beside her far away from his wife. Putting her mouth to the man's ear, this friend hissed in a passionate whisper:

"Alfred, I love you....Come, say something ....Elvira can't see us."

"Yes....Yes...." replied the girl's father, looking dreamily at his daughter as he leaned back on the gunwale, and, sighing, went on:

"It really is a beautiful day. A glorious day.... And the breasts of my little Yolanda are beginning to swell. I see it, today, for the first time....Look at her, how beautiful she is!"

The man sighed again and added:

"O, how soon our children grow...."

His friend looked at the girl with hatred and bit her lips. Soon, however, she remarked:

"Yes, Alfred, yes....I think, moreover, that Elvira ought not let your daughter go out without wearing anything under her dress...."

Five minutes later the steamer came alongside the dock. Yolanda's mother had no time to dress her daughter. The passengers were already crowding on the deck waiting for the gangway to be put into position. On the dock, friends and relatives were ostentatiously welcoming the passengers.

At last everything was ready and the passengers started getting off.

First, out came Elvira and her friend, with Yolanda between them.

The girl's eyes were shining. In her right hand she held a small cage containing an exceedingly lively canary.

THE OVERCOAT

A man stood on the open quay. No sounds disturbed the morning stillness except for the cries of a few seagulls flying round and round. This man — a man in the full sense of the word — wore a long overcoat which reached down to his feet, a top hat and held an open umbrella, despite the apparent fine weather. He was a handsome man, tall and robust, who at certain times looked like an English nobleman and, at others, like a Peloponesian from Kalamae or from Pyrgos of Elia. One could say that this man had been waiting there for a century.

2

The stillness was total. The sea's surface was smooth, sparkling in the sun without folds, without waves. The few people walking on the nearby esplanade (peripatetic philosophers mostly, wearing cloaks, and young girls hurrying to their school) were unable to explain the presence of the man wearing the overcoat, and conjectured to themselves: "On a spring day, wearing such a heavy overcoat and holding an open umbrella as if it had been pouring!"

3

The silence of that moment and the perfectly cloudless weather increased their curiosity. Suddenly, a voice was heard. One of the philosophers was saying: "When man moves away from prevailing habits and traditions, he looks like a pillar of salt in the rain."

4

Another philosopher opened his mouth and said: "When a man professes to know everything and drapes himself in luxurious and ostentatiously eccentric garments, he runs the danger of an avenging punishment."

5

At that same moment, on another point of the esplanade, a blushing young girl was whispering in the ear of a young classmate: "He is the one!...He is the one!..."

6

Her companion looked at her, turning crimson. Her lips trembled. The expression on her face was like a torn veil.

7

Another philosopher — the third in a row — cried out anxiously: "O, daughters of Lot! O, pillars of salt, among beauties of Corfu!"

8

A cock was then heard crowing, immediately after which all the bells of the town tolled simultaneously. The philosophers looked at each other thunderstruck. Not one of them was right. The bells were ringing joyfully. The sky continued being clear. The man on the quay, happy, breathed deeply — so deeply that he had to unbutton the first two buttons of his long overcoat.

9

Suddenly a loud and poignant cry rang out, and the second young girl, apparently suffering from jealousy, fainted and fell on the tiled pavement.

At that same moment, the man with the overcoat closed his umbrella. He then stood to attention, turned about and returned to his home, quite at ease.

ROMULUS AND REMUS
or men afloat in a maternal bosom

The ship (a cargo boat) sails on to its destination. Light, strengthening winds cool off the hot summer voyage.

On deck a woman sitting on a stool with a baby in her arms daydreams.

A passenger, sensitive and sharp-sighted, sits on a bench, his eyes, on this side of the rail, on the young woman with the baby and, on the other side, keeping the mother and child in view, on the foamy surface of the open sea.

Shining dolphins gambol in and out of the water. The steamer rocks on the waves. The baby is rocked in its mother's bosom. The passenger continues to observe the mother and baby, at certain moments seeming agitated and impatient, at others quite calm.

The horizon rises. The horizon falls. Sometimes it looms, sometimes it gets hidden (for a moment) below the edge of the deck.

The wind whistles through the masts, in harmony with the creaking of the wooden frame.

The sun shines.

The mother daydreams.

Suddenly the baby starts howling and its mother (a dolichocephalic woman) lifts it up in her hands, talks to it, but is unable to calm it.

The passenger studies the young woman and her baby, a wild hope seizing him....There are breasts like oranges. There are breasts resembling pears. There are breasts which look like hopes.

The baby continues to wail. Vainly does its mother try to pacify it.

The passenger's hopes increase.

The baby wails still more.

At last, its mother makes up her mind. She swiftly pulls out a breast and gives the nipple to her child. The baby grabs it and sucks it avidly.

The passenger suddenly stands up.

The horizon rises.

The horizon falls.

The sparkling dolphins dive in and out of the sea.

The baby sucks passionately. The mother gazes at the child. The sun shines. The wind sings and whistles. The baby sucks with ineffable pleasure.

Slowly, the passenger approaches from behind.

Suddenly he bends over the woman and pulls her other breast out.

There is a cry. No one hears. The passenger stoops still lower and takes the other nipple in his mouth. A second cry is heard. But the passenger persists.

No other protest is heard. Why should it be? The sun shines. The dolphins keep skipping. Powdery foam sprays up from the waves. Why should the young woman protest? Why should she complain? Three people are enjoying themselves. No one sees them.

The mother abandons herself, sighing.

Love is delicious.

Life is lovely.

INSTEAD OF AN EPILOGUE

That same night the young woman received the unknown passenger in her cabin. Whenever the child woke she took it to her bosom. But the man would not leave. Why should he leave? In pleasure, there are many positions. Love is delicious. Life is lovely.

ASPECTS OF FAIR WEATHER

To Odysseus Elytis

Himeros, on the hilltop, sounds the baptismal
fonts. He tames, and is tamed, in the pure,
unswampy bruises of everyday events and jubilees.
The sea pants and throbs before him. The cranes
ascend. The cranes descend and Himeros holds the
drumsticks in his hands and sounds the baptismal
fonts. The town pours forth over the sandy beach
to see the one who stands dominating the hill. No
blemish. No grudge. A thousand shepherds' flutes
echo the rustle of the wind.

In their classroom, before their teacher, eight girls
are silent. They are named: Merope, Nausica, De-
spo, Marina, Corinna, Flora, Leto and Melpomene.
Four hours have passed. Four hours of inexplicable
silence broken only now and again by the bang of a
door. The teacher still moves her lips but words are
inaudible. The girls continue their silence. The
meaning of the silence is incomprehensible. It is,
however, as crystal-clear as fair weather in spring at
the ruins of Corinth, when the snow-covered

mountain peaks of Roumeli resemble a vision of bliss in which the voice of a young girl is heard calling to her sister, or a lamb's bell as it idly grazes on camomile.

The sun is bright in the firmament. However, a beautiful woman consents to light the wick of a lighthouse. The lighthouse keeper approaches her and caresses her breasts. Fair weather floats on the distant horizon. A ship is immobile a mile away. The sailors do not speak. They gesture now and then and the boatswain outlines, with his right index finger, the child's name on the snow-white sails of the bowsprit. They all call him Arim-Ennis, but no one knows his origin.

Pale seashells, mingling with the steps of hotblooded Laplanders, surround Alcmene. Her home is made radiant by tufts of hovering light. Body to body, like a herd of white buffalos, clouds traverse the sky, seeming to be traveling both in and out of time. The window opens suddenly, admitting the roar of an approaching avalanche falling and rolling like a waterfall. A gust of wind thrusts the curtain aside. Alcmene is standing in the room. The Laplanders sigh and, while fair weather reigns, a crater is being formed and towers high up across the valley, on the top of the mountain.

"Northland," "Sumatra," "Corfu" or perhaps "Torrid Zone." Whatever the name, it is certainly a schooner with a tiller instead of a steering wheel in the stern. This vessel is white and the sea shudders and slides, convulsively squirming before it.

I pronounced the word sea and, at once, the knots melted in me, like the knots of those who sing: "White bird, fast sailing boat...." The waves are white, white is the erect bow of the ship which sails over the abyss of time, like the minds of ecstatic men. White bird, fast sailing boat — white feathers in the night, white waves in the sunlight, three-year-old blue colts which gambol in my mind, their red blood boiling...

The deep silent bed of the lake; above, the faultless surface. Under a dome of conjecture, or under the sun-flaming summer firmament, a stone, two stones drop in the waveless water. Suddenly the surface cracks and the lake, as if tickled, laughs in circles.

One day, two days....One day, sooner or later, it will be disturbed again like the day before yesterday, like yesterday, and a brigadier, arriving at a gallop, will stop here, as any passer-by may stop to listen to a bird or to the sudden thud of a meteor falling in a velvet forest. He will see the circles made on the surface by the stones — one moment, two moments — before stooping down to drink from the lake. He will (a mighty brigadier at that, exhausted by the long ride) bathe in the lake and never, but never forget its delights, this voluptuously rippling lake with the fathomless depth, this lake resounding with laughter.

The becoming of every myth is a child growing up. For instance, a man sees a girl holding a bird in her hand. In her other hand this girl holds a mirror and can see the man watching her hold the bird in her hand. Her hair is blonde but turns red while she is looking in the mirror and each hair shines in the sun so brilliantly that it is quite impossible to hear the noises from the road. You can only hear the words which she utters, as if she had been standing on the bridge of a steamer calmly sailing up the Oregon or the Orinoco. The natives turn dumb before her beauty, but only temporarily. One of her gestures provokes them beyond all limits of patience or control, and (inhabitants of forests or Indian nomads of the prairies) they start shouting: "Iou! Iou! Meha! Laha!" — and other similar words, words of passion and lust, while dancing erotic war dances that are absolutely irresistible. The man married the girl next day. Their son is now growing up creating myths with birds which resemble the plants of Brazil.

They all called her Oklahoma. Since she was a child she had always liked fast rhythms and broad songs resembling wide valleys traversed by bison and herds of horses from Texas and Arkansas. Perhaps this is the reason why she became a dancer so young in "The Green Island" bar. Perhaps that is why she can sing "Let us go brothers to the East" so well and "O, Adelaide, if I could only be forever near you!" among such a conglomeration of races. Perhaps this is the reason why, unlike most of her friends, she does not take up with the richest, but makes, instead, for the tough and brave men who know how to ride horses and beautiful girls. Perhaps that's why she never works under an assumed name, but always gives, in life and on stage, only one name, her real one, Oklahoma.

Birds without feathers, naked birds, bloodthirsty birds, birds flying over thickets like gigantic bats. Mute birds, fleshy birds. All the leaves are motionless in the great heat of the sun. Heavy drops of blood drop slowly on the soil. A giraffe which had been rocking its head over the trees, now drags it on the ground. Three roebucks are in the throes of death in the bushes. No voice, no help. Neither man nor lion. Fleshy birds.

Behold an orator with nasal voice. He talks continuously and now and then sneezes — like a sick whale. In front of him open *décolleté* dresses, breasts freed of their brassieres, spilling comfortably about. By way of the openings in the dresses, the men's thoughts, from the very beginning of the speech, roam among the absent-minded daydreams of the women and of the girls. The hall is full. The orator is a narcissist delighting in his own voice. But no one pays any attention. Ostrich feathers on hats and dotted or plain veils flutter and wave each time a head turns, every time a fan opens.

Fair weather, fair weather, with kites rising in the air, defines today. The town is bathed in sun and the stones around the houses that are still being built in certain quarters resemble dice which never know anything but only their own luck. The truth is that this town has always been lucky, pure and attractive. The walls of the houses are white. The sky is blue. The leaves of the trees are green, indeed so green that shadows are not discernible except as color. In the park, children let their hoops fall to the ground and with unrestrained joy, fountains of "O's!" and "Ah's!," watch their kites pull and leap in the air. Yes, this town's luck is whiter today than ever before and everything — flesh, earth, stones and leaves is — how shall I say it, how shall I say it, my Sweetest Spring — a single and indivisible delight exulting and throbbing in the sun.

The light gets stronger and stronger and in a little while noon is over. Shops and schools close and people retire to their homes. Many close the shutters and pull down the blinds. On the top floor of a house, a civil servant, with all the passion of a battering ram knocking on a gate, moves with increasing speed between the thighs of a girl who wriggles convulsively. The town delights in the constantly increasing warmth and while the girl sighs voluptuously summer arrives, surging and hot.

All veils are torn. All falsehood collapses. Pulp curdles on the scorched earth and echoes of battle crystalize. The spear piercing the ground marks the end of a complete epoch and the budding of an era only now begun. The girls' baskets are full of legends. Many of them will be remembered forever like the breasts of women and of girls that have been caressed. I hold, then, those girls' breasts and joyously triumphant, shout down the century: "All deceit has vanished. Woe, to the defeated!"

I say, now, Mercedes, I say Ariadne, because I am urged on by my lyrical vigilant metal-plated soul. When the inhabitants of Pindos finally arrive, even if they are in deadly discord with the chiefs and elders of the Saracatsanei, the women of the plains of Thessaly and the girls of Drapetsona will start a dance around me. All the choruses will mention the buffetings of Fate and the small adopted children, named by some "Alasvir," and by others "Small

Cherries," whose ripeness and maturity is certain. I feel, though, that they will say: "Well, now, why Mercedes? What is Ariadne doing here? What are these chiefs, the Alasvir, the girls and the small but sure cherries?" My answer is: The Saracatsanei are equivalent to the rising level of the water in a cistern. The mature women of the plains of Thessaly are the mothers of children who equate the greatest sorrows with the open seas, the dreams of a thousand people and of a thousand impostors rocking together. Mercedes is a Co Ltd, perhaps in Hanover, perhaps in Mecklenburgh, and the girls of Drapetsona are a kind of fruit growing everywhere, amidst toys and tins as well as under branches of trees, in whose shade irresistible children, called by some "Alasvir," and by others "Small but sure Cherries," play, especially when, taking the nipple between their lips, they suck the milk from the breasts of any Alcmene, Corinna or Ariadne.

EVENTS AND I

APHRODITE

That night, I had been looking at the stars, the constellations; I thought, however, of the day. You
looked at me in its light, beloved, rosy, lightly
dressed, and every now and then you dreamed, increasing the bright flood of light in me.

And still, outside, was night. But what a night!
A night loaded with miracles, a night pregnant with
spells.

I had been looking at the stars, the constellations, but I was seeing You at the same time. Behold! there's Sagittarius, I was saying, and Capricorn, Sirius and Orion. But I was seeing You all
the time.

Beloved, rosy, lightly dressed, you stood in me
in a luxurious flood of light. Sometimes you leaned
your head to the right and sometimes to the left,
with Orion and Sirius in your hair and Sagittarius
in your heart.

I had been looking at the stars, the constellations. Behold! there's Sagittarius, I was saying,
Capricorn, Sirius and Orion. But all the time I was

seeing You.

Beloved, rosy, lightly dressed, you had been sitting on a chair within my heart, in an incredibly bright flood of light, your shadow sometimes on the right, sometimes on the left. But you yourself were motionless, simple, sweet, most beautiful, sitting on your chair in such a manner that I was tempted to take you on my knees, one hand upon your breasts, the other underneath your dress, between your thighs.

And I was saying over and again: Behold! there's Sagittarius, look at Capricorn, Sirius and Orion; and I was always looking both at the constellations and at You.

This time, though, you were lying down — completely lying — hair spilling in the air. My hand caressed you. Your eyes talked to me. And I kept saying over and again: "Behold! there's Sagittarius, look at Capricorn, Sirius and Orion," but I could only see You now.

A wonderful miracle happened then. All the stars were extinguished and You alone remained in the sky, with me, in an eternal day and by my side. I looked at you in exaltation and I repeated your name endlessly.

And You?

You, sweet one, my Virgin full of grace, were holding, in your hands, my heart.

MADONNAS
or the ladies of the cities

I remember that we were all going madly through
our pockets.

I was in about the middle of a row of six men
who stood facing five women and a girl of about 15.
Nobody could explain our presence there nor the
reason for the inspection.

The five women and the girl were looking at us
with anxious impatience. The first two wore winter
dresses with furbelows and huge velvet hats. The
second three, wearing summer dresses, with tight
corsets, laces, and very large straw hats on their
heads, were raising their skirts slightly so that the
lower part of their legs, their pointed boots and fine
net stockings could be seen. The girl standing exactly opposite me wore a rose-colored velvet short
pelisse and a long green skirt, like Queen Amelia of
Greece. On her head, however, she was not wearing
the fez customary in those days. Beautiful loose
blonde hair fell right and left on her shoulders, and
between her breasts, casting a purple light, was a
scarab-studded hibiscus.

We were in a Pompeian hall decorated with authentic erotic murals.

Suddenly, one of us cried:

"Tallow!"

I immediately opened my mouth and shouted out triumphantly:

"Allah! Allah, is on our side!"

At once we all stopped searching through our pockets and fell on our knees, each one of us before a woman.

"My God, what beauties the world has!..." I thought, raising my eyes to the girl.

At this, the girl, exulting, gazed passionately at me, raising her skirt up to her waist, in front.

NERONE

Everyone was saying whatever came into his head.

Someone kept repeating the word "bunch."

Someone else was saying emphatically:
"O, men of Athens!"

A third one insisted on a hearing:
"The stevedores and the gladiators have
rebeled....The stevedores and the gladiators
have rebeled...."

A group of men were shouting frantically:
"Poplius Cornelius Scipion! Scipion the African!"
The lictors turned and shouted:
"Shut your traps!"
The populace replied:
"Shit!"

The commotion that ensued was tremendous.

Suddenly, something happened to startle the big

crowd that had been flooding the Coliseum since morning.

Naked, her hair stylishly combed and set with hyacinths, erect, smiling and beautiful, the Empress Poppaea entered the arena on a chariot drawn by twelve virgins of the eastern provinces. Her lips and the nipples of her breasts were dyed with blood and orange blossoms whitened her pubic hair.

The populace was shouting loudly.
I, standing on my tier, cried:
"Hail, Poppaea!"

At the same moment, the gate of the wild beasts opened and a second chariot rushed into the arena, a larger and heavier chariot than the first. This chariot was drawn by six lions from Atlas and Nubia, their reins held by Nero, crowned with roses, calm and godly in the midst of the groans and moans, in the midst of the Christians who were being burned!

The populace, exultant, was shouting loudly and

triumphantly:

"We salute you, Augustus! We salute you, Emperor!"

I, from my seat, still standing, was now shouting:

"Hail, Caesar! Mighty enemy of the Christians, hail!"

Then, Nero turned to me and raised his right hand.

At that moment, I almost went mad. Emperor Nero was I!

MADALENIA

Those who think they know everything may be interested in this story.

I was lying under the shade of a chestnut-tree. While trying to get to sleep, after a long walk, I kept saying: "Sleep, baby, sleep Madalenia! Red-faced dwarfs slip around, with black beards, unshaven beards."

But sleep did not come. Only a light breeze came in which spring perfumes floated. Although there were no crickets yet, I felt as if the whole atmosphere teemed with their vibrating chirping. A stream purled near by. The treading of the coming summer could be heard from a distance.

The hour was full of sweetness and so was my fatigue. As usually happens with those who want to go to sleep, I was tossing about trying to find a comfortable position on the ground where I was lying, constantly invoking sleep. Suddenly, I felt as if I were falling, not in a frightening way, as in nightmares, but softly and pleasantly, in a garden of Andros, my homeland, where, in spring, the lemon trees scatter their fragrance with such insistence and intensity that it floods, not only the air, but even rooms that are tightly shut, even the deepest chests of drawers, under the long, round beams which are made of cypress timber.

The comparison which I have drawn has greater significance than one may at first think. Because, I was lying not under a chestnut-tree near the village of Lamyra or Strapurges, but, as if having rolled down from slope to slope, I was at Nimborio, on one of the beaches of Andros, not far away from Plakoures, the port where, as in that other area, Riva, the Embiriceika, that is, the dwellings of the ancient and powerful family of the Embiricos who have always controlled the fortunes of that beautiful island stand silently, one next to the other, sleepless guards of the homeland, mythically enchanting to us.

As soon as I stopped rolling down, I got to my feet. Standing on the sand, I watched the morning star set, almost like the eyes of a woman in voluptuous rapture, and day gradually appeared in the sky. On my right, the town of Andros was still asleep. On my left, the road to Stenies, the largest maritime village of the island, was deserted. I remember that the smell of lemon trees was very strong; very strong and indescribably marvelous. I remember that, at that moment, I had the kind of thoughts men often have, but which they almost always conceal. How beautiful, I was thinking, it would be if a tender young girl happened to walk by, or a crisp young woman, and I caught them and, whether they wanted it or not, raped them on the shore, under the light of Aphrodite, or in a garden, near the road, breaking through their maidenheads and penetrating deep inside them, while cocks crowed on fences and figs dripped their milk on fig trees.

But no young girl and no young woman were passing by. So, on fire with lust and not knowing what I was doing, I took out my pipe and, biting it in frenzy, turned toward the sea and lit a match. It was only then I noticed that a ship, anchored about two hundred yards away from the shore, was not an ordinary sailing boat, but a large clipper of about 1,000 tons, the kind that sailors do not see today, but may find only in pictures and books, a clipper of immense beauty, exactly like those that used to ply between England and India in the nineteenth century. Its sails were half drawn. It looked as if it had only arrived a moment ago. However, no one moved on deck. Only one lantern shone on the foremast, like Aphrodite in the sky. I don't know why, but it seemed to me as if it were panting, only not in pain, but intensely, with overflowing life, having, I would say, a fast heartbeat. For a moment, in fact, I had the idea that, although it looked completely deserted, the whole vessel buzzed, from the waterline up to the topsail, like a proud and ecstatic beehive. My heart thumped. I suddenly heard quite clearly in the morning stillness, three, five, ten extremely languid sighs of the kind that one may hear sometimes, waking in the night, coming from adjoining rooms, in houses or hotels. This ship seemed to me as if it were alive. This ship made my veins race. An irresistible desire to go near it immediately overcame me. I had to reach it by whatever means. So I ran back to Plakoures, jumped into one of the slumbering boats alongside the wharf, and started rowing like a madman.

From then on, things moved quickly. Soon, I had reached the clipper and, rowing more slowly now, I circled it. This pitch-black vessel, looking as if it had given itself up to the water's caressing, was really terrific. Something urged me towards it. What did I mean to do? Why did I want it so?

Now I had reached the slender bow curved and sharpened like a sickle and I was handling the oars in such a way as not to be carried off by the current. Having secured myself, I raised my eyes. I was speechless. I was looking up at the wooden figurehead, one of those traditional figureheads representing a beautiful mermaid, under the bowsprit, that are forever breasting the waves, with raised, full breasts, blonde hair, blood-red lips and huge blue eyes gazing far over the horizon. This mermaid was a girl of breathtaking beauty. Suddenly my heart leapt almost into my mouth: "My God!" I cried out in amazement. The mermaid was breathing! Her breasts moved up and down, her eyelids opened and closed, and the sweetest sighs came from her lips. The beautiful mermaid was not made of wood. She was alive. And, along with the up and down movement of her breasts, the sides of the ship blew in and out breathing, her mouth sighing at the same time in perfect harmony. I suddenly understood why I desired this feminine ship so much. I wanted to get on it, not as a passenger but as a stallion, even before my desire had become conscious. I don't know why, but I was feeling on the threshold of eternity and looking, insatiably and lustfully, at this otherworldly apparition emerged from the sea, like primeval life out of dark chaos. A violent shudder shook my whole body. I was no longer feeling like one person but like some chosen people facing a new world.

"Aphrodite!" I cried ecstatically.

The mermaid, with a movement that had me crying out, lowered her head toward me and said:

"Not Aphrodite...Madalenia."

I looked round to my right and left at the metal name plates extending from the bows beyond the mermaid's waist. Large bronze letters, oxidized by seafaring, revealed the ship's name. This eager vessel breathing continuously through the mermaid was called Madalenia!

Before I could recover from my surprise, a clatter of feet rang out, as if lots of small children were running on the deck deserted a moment ago, while variously pitched and uncontrollable laughter burst out right and left. Ten to twelve dwarfs, redfaced and black-bearded, wearing pirate costumes of the seventeenth and eighteenth centuries, with black kerchiefs on their heads and glittering cutlasses stuck in their waistbands, were laughing wildly at me. Still laughing, one of the dwarfs said:

"You woke up very early today, Madalenia."

Another dwarf, also laughing, added:

"Sleep, baby, sleep then, Madalenia...."

While they were all laughing, a third dwarf, slightly taller than the rest, turned to me and said laughing:

"We started from the Indian Ocean and we are buccaneers....But we lost our captain and so we anchored here, at this island so renowned for its sailors, in order to take one of you on as our captain....If you want to have Madalenia, come and be our leader....Only in this way will you make her yours."

I had already made up my mind. Letting go of the oars, I stood up in the boat and, as if I were a huge ape, jumped. I found myself clinging to the live mermaid, embracing her with arms and legs.

"Raise the anchors!..." ordered the slightly taller dwarf who was the boatswain of the pirate ship. Next, he cried out loudly:

"Madalenia, the clipper sails to India today....Hurrah for our new leader!"

The laughter stopped at once and the chains immediately started rattling. I was kissing Madalenia madly. I kissed her all over, her breasts, hair, eyes, all of which were damp with sweet brine. But the moment I kissed her on the mouth, the sweetness of the kiss was such that my hands slipped off her body and I fell with a loud splash into the water.

So far, so good. Everyone will rightly agree that I had been dreaming. But what will they say when they read the following lines, when they hear the rest?

When I awoke and struggled up from under the chestnut-tree at the roots of which I had lain to rest, I took a few steps forward still under the spell of my dream. I saw, then, at the first turn in the road, a statue made of plaster, its pedestal rising out of the grass, that I had not noticed before. The statue was a copy of Aphrodite of Mylos, a perfect copy, only on a smaller scale. Automatically, I recalled my exclamation on seeing the live mermaid of the dream. I went over and stood opposite the plaster image rising among the grass. My heart suddenly leapt and I was as if transfixed. Someone had carved on the pedestal of Aphrodite, with a penknife, the name: Madalenia!

JUNGFRAU

or the echo of the beauties

To Antoni Vousvounis

The people of the mountains went down to the plains. The "Kulm," the "Rigi-Kulm," the "Alpenberg" and the "Souvretta" had emptied. The snow on Munch, Jungfrau and on Eiger, on Matterhorn and Gotthard, as on all the mountain-tops of the Engadine, turned rosy in the morning and rosy again in the evening. But the season had ended and the mountains, relieved of the crowds of visitors, breathed freely.

I was the last one left. I did not know what to do, whether to stay on the mountains this year, or go down to the plains.

I hesitated.

It was not easy for me to come to a decision straight away.

Every now and then, avalanches slid here and there in the emptiness. The rolling of each avalanche sounded, in the absolute silence of the Alpine landscape, like distant thunder, or like the heavy tread of giants.

Mountains, like plains, have a fascination of their own, their own secrets. Proof: the irresistible attraction of the tops, the tombs of the mountain climbers, the tenderness of the edelweiss among the ruggedness of the great titans.

Yes! Yes! The fascination of the mountain tops!

But plains have their own fascination too: the vast expanse of the open country; the green or blonde waves of the vast wheatfields; the triumphant procession of rivers; the mystery of secret gardens; the glory of a town basking in the sun; the sudden charge of wild horses; all the flowers of the prairie.

I did not know what to choose.

My situation was difficult, very difficult.

I decided to play the noble echo-game. If the echo was single, I would go down to the plains. If it were double, or triple, I would stay on the mountains, or rather with the mountains.

So I stuck my alpenstock in the ground, formed my palms into a loudhailer round my mouth and cried:

"Tymphrestos!"*

Something quite extraordinary happened.

Across from me, in the absolute silence, a girl appeared with long blonde braids, wearing a snow-white blouse and an all-green skirt. Cupping her hands round her mouth like I did she answered three times in a clear, sustained voice.

"Jungfrau....Jungfrau....Jungfrau...."

So, that year, I remained on the mountains.

---

* A mountain in central Greece.

HERMOLAOS THE MACEDONIAN

To HRH *Princess Mary of Greece*

At that time, I was Hermolaos, Hermolaos the Macedonian, wearing a pleated tunic, a sword at my side and a light shield on my shoulders.

I had no sarissa. However, in my left hand I held a long and strong staff, longer than all the sarissas of my compatriots, even greater than the glory of my renowned village which has been glorified for the bravery of its men and the incomparable beauty of its women.

I was, then, at that time, Hermolaos.

One day, I went down from my birthplace to the oracle of Delphi and there, at the entrance of the sacred site, I witnessed the birth of a lusty male infant, sound of limb and of extraordinary beauty, the coming of which had been divined by all the priestesses. Its birth, however, terrified those who were present, because, as had been foreseen unanimously by the oracles, it emerged with bright red arms and legs.

Although this infant was extraordinarily beautiful, the unexpected color of its limbs made all those who saw it apprehensive. For a few moments, no one could swallow. The witnesses to this scene, pale and awestruck, were inwardly praying, observing, speechless, what was going on.

When the child had emerged completely out of the genitals of its mother, the unhappy woman, groaning, begged anyone of us who happened to be there, to cut the umbilical cord. No one, however, dared approach, and the mother of the newborn child, wailing because of the sharp birth pains, cried in vain — in vain, because the purple arms and legs of the infant had frightened those standing around into total immobility.

So I, the only calm man in the whole gathering at that moment, pulled out my sword and, laying my staff against the side of a nearby wall, rushed towards the woman. Kneeling between her white thighs I cut the umbilical cord which still connected the child with the convulsed entrails from which it had just emerged screaming and beautiful.

At that same moment, a young woman, apparently a suppliant, who had been standing among the anxious spectators, clasping her hands on her firm breasts (they were clearly outlined, swaying under her dress), exclaimed loudly and poignantly:

"O, Gordian!…Gordian!…"

Immediately, I raised the infant over my head and, without knowing why, shouted triumphantly:

"Alexander! Alexander, the Macedonian!"

A different spirit now prevailed at the entrance to the sacred site. Those present, bemused and speechless, muttered incomprehensibly. A cry from the lips of the mother of the infant made me turn to her.

The mother of the newlyborn child was stretching her arms toward the baby repeating with anxious adoration:

"Alexander! Alexander! My child!"

It was only then that I suddenly lost my composure. I well knew that Alexander the Great was not due to be born for sixteen years. I knew that Philip was a youth — only 15 years old. I knew that Bucephalus had not yet made his appearance. But Alexander the Great had already come into the world, in my own hands, at the turn of a road and I, Hermolaos the Macedonian, standing in clear light, there, at the entrance of the Delphi Oracle, had anticipated and contrived in the future history of this man.

I did not know whether I should return Alexander to his mother, strangle him, or run away taking the Great Infant away with me.

It was a terrible dilemma. I felt the heavy burden of responsibility. The Gods, however, had pity on me, and through the mouth of Pythia, who fell, at that moment, into a trance behind the wall where my staff was still resting, ordered me to give the beautiful child back to its mother.

So, bearing no further responsibility towards the future of the Great Infant and towards other men, I did something simple. I kissed Alexander the Great and gave him back to his mother, feeling that I, his compatriot, had done my duty on this earth as one who, signing a very important letter, ends by saying, honestly and sincerely, before Gods and men, without any superfluous words:

I remain yours now and for ever.

Hermolaos, the Macedonian.

THE BRAVE MAN OF LIONVILLE

I was uncertain whether what I had learned from indiscreet talk in countries beyond the seas was absolutely true, or only a gossipy truth, and I did not know what to believe about all they said happened in Lionville, the day that man appeared in the town. When I arrived there, however, I soon realized that whatever I had been told in other countries was not only true but, in fact, short of the whole truth.

Something very odd, though, was going on. Although this man had achieved a lot that was admirable, no one, not a single one of all the inhabitants of Lionville, knew his name.

One thing, though, was certain — this man was a hero and he had done the place much good. One day he had appeared, out of the blue, at the town center, in the famous square with the statue of the lion in it. He delivered a short speech, lasting just about five minutes, and then began that extraordinary process which, today, is called, "The Swaddling Epic." It changed, from its very foundations, the life-rhythm of this beautiful town which had hitherto been in decline.

All this happened within three days. At the end of the third day, this strange man suddenly departed, without giving his name, or letting anyone know where he was going, only promising that, some time, he would certainly return.

Three months after the hero's departure, the inhabitants of the town erected a statue to him, exactly opposite the statue of the lion which adorned the central square. This statue was a perfect likeness of the hero who was very tall, robust, with a short beard, and wearing a long cloak reaching down to his feet. From this, the unknown man never parted, only taking his hands out, through the openings of the garment, when required in order to carry out his incredible feats.

After the brief but momentous "Swaddling Epic," everything changed. I could check this for myself, as I had twice visited Lionville, before the appearance of its mysterious benefactor, and I could now see the difference.

The city-scape had not altered, but everything else was unrecognizable. The houses, which used to be grey and dirty before, were now white, glittering in the sun. The street cars no longer creaked round the bends of the avenues. The men seemed more robust, stronger and more optimistic. Women wore longer dresses and had become more beautiful. Girls had done away with old-fashioned brassieres and in consequence acquired greater agility, plasticity and grace. The intellectuals (and there were many in the town) were no longer pale, nor believed that the only considerable works of literature were analytic or gloomy or only those that constituted or contained vaporous and abstract notions. The mentality of the inhabitants had completely altered. The change that had come about in all departments, including a more liberal view of society and the citizen's place in it, in such a short period, was truly enormous. How was it possible that no one should know the name of the man responsible for it?

But still, no one did. The hero had avoided disclosing it, perhaps out of modesty, perhaps for reasons of expediency — who knows? Nevertheless, I was determined to find out. My instinct was that this man must be very well known. So I began a systematic search. But my labors did not bear fruit and by the end of the third week of intense effort I had grown almost desperate.

Suddenly Chance smiled on me.

Having heard that one should expect little from her, I smiled back and told her that if she consented to help me a little, I would be willing to continue my efforts. Chance accepted. Besides, she was a charming young girl of about twenty, full of playful coquetry.

As we said, so we did.

I ran here and there at the behest of Chance who, like a favorable wind, urged me everywhere, helping me out in my difficult and often laborious task.

Finally, after I had visited, to no effect, all the official personages and wise men of the town, I decided to look among the common people.

On the first day I visited three butchers and two turners. On the second, I visited two moneychangers, two masons, three flowergirls, a greengrocer and, towards evening, a procuress.

On the following day I contacted persons belonging to other classes — that is, I called on a tragedian, a watercarrier, three musical comedy actresses, a juggler and two whores.

The day after that, I fell in love with a girl selling postcards. On the fifth day I decided to rest and concentrate exclusively on love-making, which took place in the country, in the arms of the young sales girl.

Our enjoyment was great and mutual. So was our passion. We returned to town the same night.

In commemoration of this day, the girl picked up a packet of postcards from the shelf of her newspaper stand, chose one and gave it to me.

This postcard was glossy and in color. It showed a very big man wearing a long cloak that reached down to his feet. He was standing opposite a large lion. I immediately recognized the popular benefactor and savior of Lionville and, being extremely moved by my young friend's gesture, as well as by her choice, took the postcard and kissed it.

The result was amazing. My lips being damp, when they came in contact with the cloak of the savior of Lionville they stuck on the glossy surface and, drawing away, unstuck and ripped a part of it off. Feet and powerful shins were suddenly revealed, underneath.

"What on earth" I exclaimed, and looked at my girl friend dumbfounded.

The girl turned to me and asked me what had

happened.

"The image," I told her, "continues underneath the cloak!"

"But how could it be possible!" she demanded, astonished. "I have sold at least three hundred of these cards, and nothing like this has ever happened."

"Here, look…" I told her and started to rip off the cape.

The hero was almost naked underneath. Except for a lion's skin partly covering his body, he wore nothing else.

"Great God!" I shouted.

"Christ and Virgin Mary!" exclaimed the young girl.

We shuddered together, in astonishment and emotion. With the help of Chance, we had discovered the identity of the legendary hero of Lionville. Before us, tall, magnificently strong and handsome, stood the great Hercules, the clubbearer, and, opposite him, blood-covered, strangled, its skin completely peeled off, the terrible lion of Nemea lay on the ground.

EXCELSIOR
or the rose of Isfahan

It was spring and I was in a public garden. We all knew that someone would be arriving that day, but no one knew who it was we were expecting, or the exact time of his arrival. We all felt, though, that the arrival was at hand, because the sky was exceptionally clear and all the birds sang madly. The grass was springing up everywhere — almost visibly to the naked eye. Abundant clear water splashed copiously from the fountains. The secretion of saliva in my mouth increased all the time. My heart beat violently in my broad chest.

Most people hung about in the avenues and in the big square of the town. I preferred, however, to wait in the public garden. Without knowing why, I had the feeling that I would be better off there, rather than at any other place, especially as I had chosen a small hill on which to stand, a hill situated on the outskirts of the park from whose slopes I could watch and follow the arrival.

My impatience grew, soon developing into uneasiness. In spite of this, being a passionate lover of tender young girls and charming young women, I found a way to cope with my impatience. I began a detailed study of three girls, all in a similar state to my own, equally impatient and on edge about the arrival. The three girls were extremely beautiful, their ages fluctuating between ten and thirteen. The first held a magnolia in her hand; the second, a May-bug; the third, and most beautiful, wore an azure cape, a large straw hat on her blonde head, and on her lips an enigmatic and, at the same time, enchantingly sweet smile.

A short way off from us, two governesses were sitting on a bench and discussing things together. A blind beggar nearby stretched out his cap and prayed to God that the sins of the dead relatives of passers-by be forgiven.

"I can't make out who's coming today. What do you think?" said the first governess.

"I don't know," answered the other. "He is coming though, he is coming....I am certain of it."

"Yes, he is coming! He is coming with glory and with myrrh," said the beggar, interrupting his begging for a moment.

"But who, after all, is coming? Who?" the two governesses asked the beggar with obvious impatience.

The blind man frowned for a while, then, turning his eyeless face towards the sky, replied:

"He who is expected from the East, from Isfahan."

The two governesses looked at each other amazed.

"What does Isfahan mean?" a very young boy, holding a yellow balloon tied to a string, asked his governess.

The first governess opened her mouth to answer but at that moment trumpets rang out. The governess got to her feet dumbfounded. The crowd, electrified, began to chant:

"He's coming....He's coming...."

After a while, from one end of the public garden to the other, from one end of the town to the other, loud rhythmic cheers began to go up from the assembled people.

"He's co-ming....He's co-ming...."

"He's coming!...He's coming!..." I also shouted, without, however, withdrawing my gaze, even for a moment, from the three girls, especially from the one with the azure cape.

"He's drawing near!...He's approaching!..." Two of the three girls, jumping about on the grass, were shouting enthusiastically with the crowd.

"He's coming!...He's coming!..." cried the entire population.

Only the third girl, her straw hat now on her knees, remained silent, an ardent expression on her face. She was incredibly beautiful.

"He's coming!...He's coming!..." the small boy repeated like a parrot, jumping spastically up and down. Then, turning anxiously but lovingly towards his governess, he cried out loudly:

"Quick...quick...please...I want to pee..."

The governess, however, ignored the child's entreaties. Conscientious though she was, her attention was completely drawn elsewhere. Deaf to the boy's cries, she also was waiting ecstatically for a sight of him who was expected, whose arrival was sounded on the trumpets, adding to the expectation and feeling of celebration an unmistakable undercurrent of universal eroticism.

While the young boy continued his entreaties, cheers were suddenly heard in the distance. Then, and only then, did I succeed in tearing my eyes from the young girls who, at that moment, in order to get a better view, were climbing the bench at the top of the grassy slope on which we were standing.

Overtaking them, I took up a position three or four yards in front of the bench, and looked down at the road. The cheers were closer now; they were getting louder and louder. The multitude vibrated. A detachment of policemen was trying to hold back the crowd, which was about to spill from the pavement on to the wide avenue in front of the garden.

At that moment, from an easterly direction, a glistening landau appeared, drawn by two fine horses. The coach was approaching triumphantly. The crowd was boiling over in excitement. The carriage seemed to contain someone very special. But the smart coachman, with his huge body, prevented us from making out who was inside.

The people, unable to contain themselves, were crying out:

"He's arrived! He's arrived!...Hurrah!...He's arrived!..."

In the midst of the pandemonium, the blind beggar's words came to my lips and, along with other cries, from time to time I shouted out:

"He's coming!...He comes with glory and with myrrh...."

The carriage drew even closer, until at last its passenger appeared before my dazzled eyes.

Among cries and shouts of joy, exclamations of rapturous admiration were now heard. In the landau an exquisitely beautiful young girl of 11 or 12 was standing on the back seat, all by herself, completely naked. Smiling, she graciously greeted the multitudes to her right and to her left. Her blonde hair was being ruffled in the breeze, the nipples of her young breasts were erect, while nestling between her white thighs, among her golden pubic hillock, lay, rosy, protuberant and throbbing, her tender vagina.

The people cheered and shouted with joy. I could not believe my eyes. The young girl riding in the landau was none other than the beautiful girl with the azure cape who was with us in the park only a moment ago!

Still remembering the prophetic words of the blind beggar, I cried out, my soul on fire:

"Glory be to you, Rose of Isfahan! O Beautiful One, Full of Grace, Glory to you."

Tears of joy filled nearly everyone's eyes, as well as mine. As soon as the carriage had passed, 1 turned round and looked at the bench. Only two girls stood on it. The third one, the most beautiful, was missing. Only her azure cape and her large straw hat were in her place. I ran over to snatch the hat and lift it up. Underneath lying on the azure cape was a magnificent rose. I shivered violently as I took it in my hand. A small envelope was pinned to one of its leaves. In the envelope was an extremely delicate prophylactic made of fine elastic and in it a small piece of folded paper. I took out the paper, unfolded it and read it in astonishment. At that moment, I heard someone, behind me, reading out the content of the minute note, which had been written in the handwriting of a child.

"Whoever finds me ought to keep me. I am she whom you have been expecting."

I turned round to see who was standing behind me. It was the blind beggar who had regained his sight and who was reading, over my shoulder, the precious note, the precious message which I held in my hands — I, the luckiest man in the world!

The vast crowd was still delirious.

Nearby the two governesses were kissing each other. The small boy had pissed all by himself for the first time, like a real man, and had joined in the cheering with his shrill, childish voice. A policeman, wild with excitement, was shooting in the air. A middle-aged man was kneeling under an orange tree and muttering passionate prayers accompanied by incomprehensible sighs. Men were throwing their hats in the air. Women and girls were waving their arms, crying or laughing. The blind man's eyes sparkled. I wanted to shout something again but I was so moved that I only managed to cry out, like a whinnying horse. At last, hurriedly clasping the beggar's arm, I rushed madly from the garden, taking the cape, the straw hat, the rose and the precious note with me. Running like mad, I followed the road along which the landau carrying the beautiful young girl had disappeared. A strong smell of roses issued forth from all around and the people frenziedly celebrated in the streets, fraternizing under a magnificent shining rainbow, which had unexpectedly appeared in the clear sky.

PERSONS AND EPICS

OEDIPUS REX

To Marie Buonaparte

It is time the truth was told.

It will be revealed to you by a simple man of the woods, born and bred by Pan and the Amadryads.

After wandering about the plain of Athens, on the way from Boetia, King Oedipus and I, the huntsman Havrias, finally arrived at Colonus. The blind ruler of Thebes, panting and heavy, his eyes still bleeding, leaned on my shoulder and, with the assistance of a stick, followed me, groaning because of his physical and mental suffering.

We had been walking for two days and two nights, and now, at the beginning of the third day, early in the morning, I descried, in the dazzling Attic light, the temple of the Eumenides. I was helping Oedipus as best I could, supporting him under the armpit, but the poor king, in spite of his superhuman efforts, could only drag himself along. Besides his other sufferings, his feet had become swollen again.

Whatever I write here, you must realize, is done

specifically to restore the truth, since certain facts concerning the last moments in the life of the king of Thebes, as recorded by historians and tragedians, are totally inaccurate. I am in a position to prove my facts and I shall proclaim them as loudly as I can because, as you will see, I was a witness to those tragic events.

Oedipus was not taken to Colonus by his daughter Antigone. His beautiful daughter only led him as far as Cithaeron where she came upon me and my three dogs on my way back from hunting. She begged me to accompany her slow-walking father to Attica. The reason for this was that, afraid the old man might sooner or later commit suicide, she wanted to get to the temple first, so as to propitiate the Eumenides and sweeten the king's life after death.

I agreed to take Antigone's place at her father's side, and the beautiful girl, hurrying to Colonus with Mercya, one of my three dogs (whom I ordered to follow her so as to protect her on the way), arrived at the site near Athens a long time ahead of us.

I shall never forget the blind martyr's agony as he dragged himself along at my side. When, groaning, he described to me the shattering story, I, the simple man of the woods whose main God and protector is Pan, repeatedly tried to console him by telling him that the fact that he had a love relationship with his mother Jocasta, did not seem so terrible a thing to me, adding that I would have done the same and that, if I begot daughters by her or another woman, I would gladly sleep with them, too. Nor, though they would be at their most tender age, would I feel any remorse. In support of my arguments I mentioned the Olympic Gods who carried on love affairs of this kind almost daily. But the unfortunate king, swearing and cursing himself for what had happened to his family, was past consoling, though I tried a second time.

"My good lord," I said, "Don't go on like this. listen to me; I am telling you the truth....Even today most men are mad....It is not right for a great king like you to get confused about things that are so simple....You have been punished and suffer unjustly....A day will come when incest will be considered as normal as the other kinds of love and then, when no man will any longer fear his father, will he need to kill him. Men and love will at last be free, like we are, the simple, healthy men of the woods...."

I wanted to add: "Only those who want to be blind cannot see this." Thinking, however, that this might be construed as irony by the blind king, I desisted.

However, as soon as Oedipus heard what I had said, he fell to even more violent recriminations and despair.

Realizing that what I was saying, as an honest and sincere man, not only did not succeed in lessening the king's grief and pain but, on the contrary, was aggravating it, I gave the subject up and remained silent.

At last, after a good deal of wandering about (I must admit that I was not familiar with the country beyond Cithaeron), we reached Colonus.

Here I was fated to be the witness of a scene which I will always remember with abhorrence and horror. O, if I had only had the power to make Oedipus listen to me! He would be alive today, revered and happy.

Antigone — who was not merely beautiful but also a good daughter, who loved her father and brothers — was awaiting us at the top of the temple steps. As soon as she saw us, she ran joyfully to greet us, my good Mercyas at her heels.

"Father! Our good Havrias!" she exclaimed and after she had kissed the king who could now barely stand, added: "Father, I have succeeded in propitiating the Eumenides!...They will be lenient...."

Thankfully, I turned Oedipus over to his daughter and left them, saying that I wanted to rest. The truth is I had been greatly attracted by the beautiful girls of Attica who I had met on the way. Having no hesitations whatsoever of the kind the king of Thebes had, I decided to capture one, or even two of them and taking my dogs along took to the fields.

My search met with success. My erotic prey (two girls working in the vast olive grove of Attica) was rewarding, and after two hours, replete and happy, I returned to Colonus.

Alas! what a horrifying sight awaited me! The three Furies had deceived all three of us, Antigone, her father and me. At the propylaea of the temple, while Oedipus, the blind king of Thebes, lay full length on the tiles, yelling and struggling, and Antigone, kneeling and bare-breasted, tore her clothes in her grief, the hateful Eumenides, vilely revengeful despite the dazzling Attic light, were involved in indescribable atrocities. With subhuman cries and grimaces, Aleto and Megaera held the unhappy martyr down and Tissiphone bit at his genitals with her teeth, tearing them away like an hyena.

So, I, Havrias the simple huntsman of the Boetian woods, but a good archer, taking upon myself to be universal conscience, avenger and punisher, tore the bow from my back. Taking three sharp arrows from my quiver, I drew taut the string of my bow and killed the three Eumenides.

Unhappily the castration had already taken place and Oedipus soon died. The tragedies that followed are well known. But, at least, the three miasmas of this world no longer existed and my good dog Mercyas, along with my two other dogs, tore the corpses of the Furies to bits and destroyed all evidence of them.

I report all this so as to get the record straight. Because, the fact is, whether through bad faith or in pure ignorance, historians and poets, when they write about the last moments of King Oedipus, simply waffle.

NEOPTOLEMOS A
King of the Hellenes

pages from a diary

Today is the third anniversary of my departure from the lunatic asylum and once again I recall, with the deepest feelings, the time when I was mad! What an adventure! Even if I lived to be a hundred, I should remember this period and that good man who stood by me with such affection, devotion and courage throughout my illness. Happily all this belongs to the past and, celebrating today, once more, the full restoration of my mental health, I praise God and feel grateful to the man who became his assignee in order to save me.

How can I help but go over certain incidents from that period! What made the greatest impression on me, was the discovery that men not only use reason but that they go down on their knees before it. I did everything in my capacity to persuade them that they were wrong; not only by my daily behavior, but with lectures, speeches, articles in magazines and newspapers and sometimes (three times in all) by violently attacking a statue of extraordinary beauty, done by a sculptor I knew, who had the unfortunate idea of calling his beautiful work, "Reason." All my attempts, though, were in vain. They finally got me and shut me up in an asylum where, for years (four altogether), I continued my struggles to no purpose.

In this institution, with a few exceptions, the doctors were reasonable but morons — that is, they were mentally on a much lower scale than many madmen. The most outstanding person there was the man who saved me — who, anyway, was not an ordinary psychiatrist, but a psychoanalyst, an imaginative psychoanalyst at that, as is shown by his interpretations as well as by his literary works.

When I was taken to the asylum, I wore a samovar (my mother's samovar) on my head in the manner of a helmet. I had fastened it with a strap under my chin and I roamed round the streets holding a lance in my right hand, at intervals shouting as loudly as possible:

"Dioscuros! Pity on others and on ourselves!" (I had read the phrase in one of the writings of my psychoanalyst whose work I admired and knew by heart). For this reason, and because I always added, under my signature, without really knowing why, the beautiful pen-name "Neoptolemos" (a name with which I was glorified and by which I also glorified contemporary Greek literature), the doctors of the asylum from the start called me Neoptolemos. I am of the opinion that this was the only clever thing those poor fellows did throughout my stay at their institution.

Four years! Four years of confinement for a pure genius who came to this world to serve poor humanity. (I use this phrase in the same way that a Peloponnesian patriot, under the Turks, would say: "Poor, poor, Moreas!") But now here I am, cured, completely cured and I want to thank you, once again, almighty God and you, my most devoted and kind doctor, for extending your strong and generous hands so affectionately and protectively over my head and my soul....

Man is the greatest mystery in the world. One day he is like clay on which his will molds what he wants; another day he is like clay on which, however, it is the gaping, bottomless, abysmal unconscious and not his will, that controls him, giving him expression and form, forcing him to do this or that without being aware of it. Only genius can provide solutions that are really conclusive. O, how great and admirable is this "entelechy." And God has blessed me with this entelechy giving my genius free rein. Because I really feel that I am a genius; as long as I am not hit on the head by a tile; as long as I am not stabbed slyly by this or that enemy, or by one of those secret or public gangs which commit crimes supposedly in the name of suffering humanity.

O, my pure blood, my rich and warm sperm! You, who have raised me, like tropic whirlwinds, to the highest peaks of the Universe! I owe you everything. Because you, my priceless and liquid Porphyra and you, my divine erotic Galaxy, are God in me, and I, through You, bring Him to the others, the small and the great, the happy and unhappy. O, you, my throbbing carotid, O, you, my ever-throbbing erect penis, I owe everything to you because you are, organically and in your original substance, the God who always comes to those who can really believe. O, lance, my lance, my golden lance, and you, red jug, my heart, I write with you, the oath of victory or death, of squirming, convulsive carnal delights, the oath of all life, from the Acroceraunia mountains to towering Tolima, from Mekka, my love, Allah, to the high plateaus of Asia, from Mississippi and Missouri to the Amazon and Zambezi, from the depths of the Pacific to the lofty peaks of the snow-covered Cordilleras.

Yes, yes, I am indeed a genius. How can I hush up the fact that the only progress will be through the geniuses of this world, among whom I hold a prominent position (I thank you again, my God and my doctor), I, the ex-madman, today sane, but equally a genius then and now, I, Neoptolemos, the son of the renowned Achilles, the glory of Hellenism and of Islam, glory of the presence of yesterday, of today, of tomorrow and of all time, the glory of the eternal presence.

My beloved, glorious father, Achilles, the time soon approaches when I shall take revenge on all your enemies, at the Delphic Oracle. O, Hellas, my beloved and sweet mother, the time quickly approaches when I shall impregnate you, whether you want it or not, I, Neoptolemos, your handsome offspring, destroying all plots against you once and for all, founding a new era, for the benefit of the Universe and for the glory of the Hellenes.

My dearest brothers, I have at last become a man! Listen to me....All of you....Young and old. I said, I have become a man. I am 3,000 years old. I bear in me the entire history of Greece and the legacy of Hellenism. I entered Troy in the Trojan Horse. I killed Priam and Astyanax. My brothers....Follow me!...I am strong and powerful....I shall lead you forever into absolute intellectual and material greatness.

Almighty God! I see it now. I see it crystal clear. I see what my destiny is and my purpose. I am deeply shaken. O, what a great mystery is the becoming of things! When I sat here two hours ago to write a few words in my diary about today's third anniversary of my happy exit from the asylum, I was not yet sure what my true destiny was. While writing, though, a moment ago, I realized it and still writing, obviously moved by God's hand, I took my decision....My brothers, I bring you joyful tidings! I am a pretender to the throne of Greece. My brothers, I am telling you once and for all, without beating around the bush — I am your King! My brothers, my new career begins today.

Long live the Nation!

after one hour
As soon as I wrote the previous passage, I thought I ought to say a few words to the man who helped

me recover from my illness, to show, by an official act, how great my gratitude was. I copy this letter here, in my diary, so that, in time, it may be entered in the official State registers.

from the temporary palace
My doctor and benefactor,

Today I celebrate the third anniversary of my emergence, thanks to you and the Almighty God, from my grave illness. This day is sacred to me, not only because it symbolizes my complete recovery, but because on it, without any trace of delirium, I recognized my true destiny and took my decision, responsibly and irrevocably. Doctor, my thinking is lucid and my logic, perfect. Look, my dear, how…

Since I am Neoptolemos, I am, inevitably, the son of Achilles. Since I am the son of Achilles, I am Neoptolemos. My decision is the outcome of the above. My doctor, my dear friend, today I succeed my father to the throne of Greece, to forge her new glory and consolidate her greatness and happiness with my own hands. As I have already told you, my decision is final and irrevocable.

I am leaving tomorrow morning on the first bus in order to dynamite the Delphic Oracle. Thus I will take my revenge on Apollo for the death of my dear father. I shall then return to Athens immediately to make arrangements for my coronation.

Doctor, you see that I am quite rational both in my thoughts and in my actions; that dominant reason which you helped me to recover guides me.

In gratitude for all you did for me, I appoint you, my dear, you who have always been a sleepless frontier guard and sentry on the remotest lookout posts of the Intellect and the Empire, I appoint you, I repeat, High Commander of Greek poets and psychoanalysts and concede to you, if you so wish, Andromache.

> In Athens the 25rd of February, 1946
> Neoptolemos A´
> by God's Will King of the Hellenes

THE MAIDEN OF PENNSYLVANIA

I know it would be best not to say anything because, apart from the fact that many consider me
insane, my confession might have terrible conse-
quences. Something, however, impels me to confess
and express what I feel, *"à mes risques et périls"* (for-
give these few French words, but I am of French
origin, on my mother's side, and of English origin
only on my father's side), which I do, assuming all
responsibility. So I dip my pen in the ink and be-
gin, hoping that my sharp nib will not irritate me
unnecessarily with its terrible scratching on the paper, me, the lover, who has undergone years of torture.

The sheets hung outside the windows and the
wind made them flap, almost bluster like white
foam in cobalt blue — what am I saying, not in the
cobalt blue (this color applies elsewhere), but in the
sky blue, where angelic hymns echo....And that is
how You come now to my mind....O, God what a
mistake I made....Why do I say that you come to
my mind now; you have never left it, for you are always in my thoughts, since I always think of you,

yes, yes, forever, day and night, of you, beautiful and tender maiden of remote Pennsylvania, just as you were when you were still alive in those far-off years, a girl of twelve, as you were then, angel-like in your white dresses, with lace round the neckline and huge bows behind, on the waist, huge bows of cobalt blue....

But I must not digress....The sheets hung outside the window and if they had not been so pallid and white, if they'd had some colored stripes, they might, perhaps, have resembled the star-spangled banners of those states with the blue, red and white starry flags, the multitude of stars which I would have loved to see forming a diadem on your hair, my white angel, with your small white buttoned shoes, your azure eyes under your golden hair. But the sheets were not colored. They were white and wan and so did not bring to mind the gala days, municipal bands, gaudy ballroom dances and parades of mounted lancers. To me, they correspond to days of decay, to the cold sun of an extremely northern country, although I am from the South, the real South, born in the cottonfields of Louisiana and nursed on the warm songs of the Negroes. So, these sheets are to my soul the same as you — you, as what you finally became, since at first you were snow-white and graceful but at the same time warm, full of sap and youthful exuberance, with rosy lips and cheeks, a maybug, sometimes, in your fingers, at others, a bird, or a magnolia in your hand, your head sometimes uncovered or your broad straw hat on, with the velvet ribbon (cobalt blue), which began at the brim and hung down the straw on to your back....

However, I have forgotten what I wanted to say....But it doesn't matter....When I let myself go a little, everything comes back eventually....Everything, that is to say you, always you, my sweet maiden.

What was I saying then?...O, yes....The sheets were hanging outside the window and flapped in the wind — large, white, grand sheets looking like festive birds, or like the huge white wings of angels....

My beautiful angel, why should I conceal it! I really loved you passionately, in the way that ivy climbs and winds tight around the tree it loves, almost strangling it sometimes.

At first, I thought there was a hope....If nothing else, I thought that some solution could be found, the solution of secret vice or, if necessary, abduction. But it was not easy to overcome my inhibitions, to quieten or drown the voice of my conscience. I was responsible for different things. I was supposed to be your guardian and guide you, I was supposed to protect you. In this conflict I had only the privilege of your untouchable presence, the distant vision of you and your dresses — your beautiful white dresses, with a little lace round the neckline, huge bows at the back, your white gloves, the white shoes with the small buttons and your broad straw hat....Without your knowing it, I used to take all the things you wore and clasp them for hours, caressing and kissing them, especially your dresses....What else was there left for me to do, my golden angel, my darling little girl! Your sheets were added later. When in the morning the maid hung them out of the window of your country-house, I would run and substitute them for mine. So, at night, I slept in your sheets and you, unaware, slept in mine....What else could I do, my love, without raping you, without being lewd, a predatory demon at the side of an angel, at the side of a tender and exquisite maiden, with eyes of perfect stillness, and lips like paradisal rosepetals with the sweetest of sighs, to which your soul came, brimming.

O, white dresses and white sheets of my life! Velvet or silk belts with bows and ribbons always cobalt blue, leather shoes and gloves, tight and perfumed!

I invoke those clothes of yours, my sweet one, because it was only through them that I came in contact, even indirectly, with your body. You see, my love, you were only twelve then and I had not dared touch you. This torture lasted another year; a year of resistance to temptation, of the repression of my love. A real torment. But still, but still....What I said was not entirely true, because although what I felt was of course torture, it was torture with a certain sweetness — especially when we were left alone together, under the trees of your father's farm, or in the big, peaceful rooms of your sumptuous home.

My entire life centered on yours. As I watched you at your daily tasks, or lost in your enchanted private dreams, you seemed to me, not like a girl on earth, but like a young goddess, a heavenly virgin....

Yes, my entire life centered on yours; all my

fantasies, all my passions. You were everything to me. The entire creation; the rivers, the woods, the prairie; everything — earth, heaven and the Milky Way....

Until then, you had not understood anything. But at the beginning of your thirteenth year, one day when the colts jumped around the chestnut-colored mares, I looked into your eyes long and insistently. I think, perhaps, that you understood something then for the first time, my sweet child, something very vague, something very chaotic, and you blushed like a poppy, in your white dress, under your broad straw hat with the long blue velvet ribbon. I remember that you were holding a may-bug. At that moment, your fingers opened and the bug flew away and disappeared. Over our heads the sky buzzed gloriously, as if hordes of archangels were fluttering. My mind seethed, the plain's fragrance wafting up to me. Below us the colts still pranced about, and, far away in the distance, the voices of the villagers every now and then welled up like sudden oracles. I remember that at that moment a train was passing, winding through a stretch of wide prairie on the newly-constructed track of the first Pennsylvanian railroad. The white thick puffs of steam burst from the swelling funnel, floating off like clouds of erotic delight, under the vault of an azure happiness. They dispersed then, spreading over the sky like white cool sheets flapping in the sun, in our sun which so gloriously warms these blessed States.

I don't know how, but at that moment it seemed to me that a strange natural phenomenon took place, there, before our eyes; a magnificent and momentous event. It seemed to me that a tall and purple fountain suddenly spurted from within the grass, close to the trunk of a felled oak, on which we had been sitting. You raised your eyes, having only just lowered them under my persistent gaze, and looked dumbly at me. It was then I understood that what I had thought to have been an outward natural phenomenon had not occurred outside me, but only in me. My own feelings were the source of this fountain, while my heart beat like a drum at battle time. I, the Southerner, the old Catholic of Louisiana, felt like crying out, emitting a war-cry which would, at the same time, be a prayer, like the triumphant shouts of the warriors of Islam. Not knowing, though, any of the invocations of the believers in Allah, I cried in our own liturgical language: "Glory! Glory! Halleluia!" and I bent and kissed you on the mouth for the first time.

O, how deeply did you sigh! How sweet the taste of your lips! Although you were innocent, although you thought that I was kissing you like a mother kisses a child, you got very upset. When I removed my lips from yours, you were pale. You suddenly blushed like a poppy. Your chest heaved up and down. In fact, I think that, from that moment, your breasts started developing faster, because the two small protuberances which you had in your bosom before then became much larger and more noticeable. In a few weeks, they became much more protuberant and large like twin live balls throbbing under your dresses with your every movement — two spherical swelling globes matching the bursting roundness of your two buttocks under the big cobalt blue bows that were always tight round your lithe waist.

O, my love!...I just remember that your straw hat fell from your knees, where you held it until a moment ago, when I kissed you. Afterwards I bent down to pick it up, but I did not notice that you were standing, with one of your shoes, on the streaming blue ribbon, and as I pulled the straw hat the ribbon remained on the grass. I still keep this ribbon in a special chest, along with your dresses, your gloves and all my other treasures....

O, the happiness I felt with that kiss! I thought about it day and night. But another five or six months passed before I touched you again. And the sheets flapped every morning outside the windows of your country house. And I kept substituting them with mine, like before. And, as always, I pressed your dresses tightly to me, when no one was looking. At last, after five or six months, without any premeditation, the parlor scene took place, like a sudden flash of lightning.

It was night. The wind howled and the rain lashed the window panes. We were sitting by the lit fireplace with the white pediment and the small white columns which made it look like the propylea of your mansion. Your father was away, as usual, in Pittsburgh and this made you even more aware of the absence of your mother and of your sad orphanhood. I was sitting on an armchair, opposite yours, pretending to be reading the *Philadelphia Sun.* I was watching you embroider a teacloth with small blossoms which looked astonishingly like the bows of your dresses, the same cobalt blue. At the round table, by your side, the oil lamp with the tall glass and the big white globe shed a soft, mellow light on your face, a light like a caress. On the left of the lamp, a daguerreotype of your mother, showing her in a dark crinoline and wearing long white leather gloves up to her elbows, her arms gently resting on an Ionic pillar (with ivy climbing up it) showed how like you were to her, my love, especially about the mouth and the large dreamy eyes. But you were even more beautiful than your mother and my heart was on fire....I was watching you — O, how I watched you — thinking of the long torment when I had lived so very near you without expressing my adoration for you, without disclosing my burning desire, hushing up, hiding my feelings while the temptation grew, constantly grew in me....

The wind continued to howl and the rain beat hard on the panes. The storm raged. Suddenly it seemed to me as if we were on a deserted coast of the Atlantic, that it was not the trees that hissed around us, but the vast ocean, and that we were not sitting in the living room of your father's house but in a very tall lighthouse where my love shone in the terrible night, over the waves and the watery depths.

It was no longer possible to admit that I could go on living, as I had done up to then, in a long, quivering drawn-out torture of postponement....It was impossible to content myself any longer with embracing and kissing your empty dresses, with substituting the sheets, with loving only visually....Winter was heavy outside, but in the living room the fireplace burned cheerily and it was pleasantly warm. Behind the title of the *Philadelphia Sun*, under the big capital letters, a stylised sun spread its rays over the newspaper which dumbly, but at the same time eloquently, contained all the hustle and bustle of the universe — a great rising sun which, spreading beyond the printed paper, pricked my burning heart with its rays, as I desired to prick you....

My love, there are moments when even the most tender love becomes cruel and savage, because that is how it is meant to be, it is the nature of things. All the eagles of Colorado, the stallions covering young mares, the Red Indians of the prairies, the bison of the plains, all the frantic — that is the good — lovers know what I mean....My white angel, that night, in the warm living room of your home, while the storm raged outside you learned it too.

The space which separated your armchair from mine was, to me, Rubicon, and I crossed it. For a moment, you looked at me in amazement; then, in terror. You cried out....But I had crossed the river and nothing could keep me back any longer.....I remember that the moment you started screaming, I heard five, six, ten sharp and protracted whistlings. Through the night, as every night at the same time, the Pennsylvania Express roared heedlessly and triumphantly through the storm, undaunted, like the charge of countless mustangs, like Destiny itself.

So, my beloved, did you learn my love, and along with that you learned my other secret — my great unimaginable secret, which you kept so faithfully, and so well, my sweet.

After that, for about four months I lived in complete contentment. We stayed together day and night and every night, when the servants retired, I took you to my bedroom. There have never been happier husband and wife. Little by little, I had overcome all your fears. Your initial apprehension disappeared and, although you were a child barely 13 years old, you soon became so warm and open that even the most experienced, the most skilled daughters of Venus would have envied you.

But, in spite of our precautions, the inevitable happened. Your pregnancy began to show. At first, we did not know what to do, or what to say. We felt desperate, all the more so because we both wanted to have the child now that it existed. At last, I found a solution. When the fourth month was near we accused Jacob, the servant, who had disappeared a month earlier, having stolen two of your horses from your farm. Because of the theft, it was easier to blame the servant for the rape as well. That is what we did, cunningly taking care to attribute the lack of any protest by you, and your long silence, to your innocence.

It was in this way that we brought it to light. The few people to whom we had to tell this lie believed it completely, as, most importantly, did your father, the senator. Jacob was not arrested and, so, our lie continued to shield us. The truth was never revealed. Your father, having first dismissed me for negligence, took you away from the farm, before anyone could realize that you were pregnant, and set you up in the small house of a close friend of his, near Pittsburgh, with an old woman, whom he trusted, to look after you....

After about five months you died in that house,

my little angel, and our little child died with you, at the end of spring, at the end of my life — because, since then, I have not really lived. I only exist physically, mechanically. The only joy left to me is memory and the few souvenirs which I managed to collect and take away with me before I left your estate — two of your white dresses, a pair of shoes, two laces, a pair of gloves, your straw hat, two of your sheets, two long, cobalt blue broad ribbons (like those you used for the huge bows at the back) and something else, my love, something completely yours — some blonde hair.

Twenty-five years have passed. I never told anyone I loved you. Before today I never mentioned to a single soul that I was your lover. And I never revealed the other secret that only you knew....I do not know, though, whether I shall live much longer; I am too much bent by the years and still more by the unending pain of your loss. So now, before departing from this world, I want to reveal my secret, my white angel, my golden girl.

Thus I am writing this confession, which is like a funereal chant in minor white and cobalt blue, to let you know that I still love you and to let people know, even if I were to blame — to blame at all, dear God — that great loves do not exist only in books, but even more so in life, revealing, at the same time, through the few words which I shall add after my signature my other great secret.

LOUIS VERNON
From New Orleans of Louisiana,
known until now as Caroline Vernon,
governess.

P S I beg that I be buried, when I die, shrouded with the two sheets which have, embroidered on them, the initials A.P., next to the grave of Alberta P...., in the graveyard of Philadelphia, and to have inscribed on the white marble of my tomb, in cobalt blue letters:

LOUIS VERNON
Lover till death of the exquisite Alberta.

SAMUEL HARDING

The small red light indicating ascent went on and in a few seconds the rolling grated door of the elevator opened. Samuel Harding, the millionaire senator of Illinois, consultant of the United Slaughter Houses of Chicago Company, vice-president of the Steam Navigation Transports of Lake Michigan and president of the Union Pacific Railways Company, entered the small square space, and the descent, noiseless and fast, began.

The heart of the aged man leapt suddenly and Samuel was worried, remembering the diagnosis the heart specialists had made that morning. But it was nothing serious. His pulse became normal again and in a while the senator landed in the lobby of the basement of the large hotel where he stayed. The lobby led to the barber shops, the pool room and the room with the pin ball machines.

That day, Samuel Harding, for the first time, proceeded, not to the bar, or the other halls of the ground floor, but to the pool room, since, upstairs, the heat was unbearable while there, in the basement of the hotel, it was not only cool, but the final preliminary game for the pool championship of the United States was taking place.

No drink, no smoking, no fatigue of any sort and no kind of strong emotions — that is what the doctors had told this tall and white-haired young man. I call him "young" because Samuel Harding, in spite of his 65 years, was hearty and hale and his blue clear eyes shone behind his round gold-rimmed glasses. The deprivation of so many things was unbearable to him. However, the senator loved life and, wanting to live as long as possible, he had decided to comply — at least for a while — with the instructions of the doctors, and then....Then, it was up to God. Tomorrow, with the report of the top specialists in his pocket and having made a firm decision to abide by their orders, he would return to his own State where he would start his treatment and his rest.

Directing himself toward the pool room, Samuel had approached the entrance when a blonde young girl, about eleven years old, coming out of the room and accompanied by her governess, barred his way. Harding's heart leapt violently.

The young girl was of an extraordinary beauty. As soon as she passed him, smiling and alert, the senator turned and looked back at her, thunder-struck. This young girl looked amazingly like his daughter, Adelaide, who had been lost, along with his wife, in the course of the terrible fire which burned down the city of San Francisco and from which, as if by miracle, he alone had been saved.

The graceful child, still precociously smiling, continued on her way, together with her governess, toward the pin-ball machines. In spite of his wild heart beat, Samuel Harding, forgetting on the spot all his doctor's instructions, turned round and fol-lowed her, as if magnetized.

The truth is that the senator madly loved his lost daughter Adelaide. But it was equally true that the virile old man loved every good-looking young girl and had a special weakness for young girls be-tween the age of ten and fifteen. Age had no effect on these inclinations of his. On the contrary, with the years, his passion became stronger. This time, because of the amazing likeness between this beau-tiful young girl and his daughter, he tried to per-suade himself that he was interested in her only in a fatherly way. But as he had always been honest with himself he soon admitted that an emotion which was not solely fatherly but was at the same time intensely erotic, forced him to pursue the beautiful young creature. As if in sudden illumination, Samuel understood something else too, that is, that he had always loved his own daughter in a similar way.

The girl had entered the room with the pin-ball machines and was now standing before a large table covered with green felt. She was leaning forward and inserting a coin in a metallic slot. The coin disappeared. The child pulled a lever and then suddenly let it go. The lever, springing forward, slung out a ball. The green table was crammed with obstacles, in the shape of round holes. Each hole had by its side, on a tiny mushroom-shaped pole, the name of a city of the United States. The player won only if the ball reached the end without falling into any of the holes.

The ball started rolling on the sloping table. The senator had placed himself on the opposite side to the girl and observed her, dazzled. The ball hit the first and second poles but went around both holes and continued its descent. The young girl followed it with open mouth. Next to her the governess grinned. Samuel Harding felt his heart beating violently but kept his eyes glued on the beautiful young girl. She was almost identical with his daughter Adelaide.

The ball kept rolling downwards. The senator's pulse kept beating faster and faster. The ball hit the fourth obstacle, the obstacle of the city of Chicago, without falling into the hole, passed without accident in front of the fifth and continued its way toward the terminal, from which it was separated by ten more obstacles. Each stood for a city with a railway station belonging to the Union Pacific Company, of which, by a very strange coincidence, Harding was the president. If the ball succeeded in reaching the terminal, its fall into the special hole that awaited it would set into motion a perfect miniature train, each carriage of which bore on its sides the sign: "Pacific Express."

The rolling ball, having started from New York, had already left behind it Cleveland, Pittsburgh, Indianapolis, Chicago, Des Moines, a town of Wyoming, Lincoln, in Nebraska, and was already entering new territory. The eighth obstacle was the capital of the State of Utah, the seat of the Mormons, Salt Lake City. The ball hit the hole but did not fall into the hole. Touching for a second its slightly bulging rim, it continued on its way. A deep sigh of relief came from the mouth of the young girl. Samuel also sighed deeply. He was in perfect communion with her. The governess still kept grinning. The young girl looked at Harding for a moment and blushed. Immediately she returned her gaze to the ball which was now approaching Carson City, in Nevada. The senator's heart beat violently.

"Your desires are my desires, your joys are my joys and your worries, my worries, my angel," said Samuel, to himself. His penis bulged, elongated, taking, under his underwear, the dimensions and hardness of a full erection.

The governess raised her purse to her eyes as if to conceal her broad smile but she continued to observe the senator's penis as it throbbed under his trousers. The senator did nothing to hide his state. On the contrary, he wished the girl to see what her beauty had done to him. But the girl saw nothing. All her attention had been absorbed by the ball, which was approaching Carson City, and she watched it, thrilled. Suddenly the ball hit the metallic rim of the hole, darted slightly outward, and seemed as if it would continue its course on the green table. But its momentum was not sufficient to carry it over the slight depression of the hole and, rolling backwards again, it fell inside once and for all.

Up till now, every time the ball passed the obstacles successfully, Samuel Harding felt, along with the young girl, not only relief and joy but also something which seemed like glee, something like prelude to an oncoming victory. In fact, the last two times he thought, "Surely, surely I will be cured; I will be all right in a couple of months...." Now, on the contrary, now that the ball had fallen in the hole, he felt inside him something like a hard blow, something like an implacable blow of destiny. Not only for himself, but also for the beautiful young girl who, having exclaimed sadly once or twice, was now looking in silent despair at the ball coming to rest in the hole.

Who knows — thought the senator — what hopes this pink-blonde angel had placed on the turn of the game.

Who knows what wishes, what desires, what longings escorted this ball with all the force of her little heart. Who knows with what omens, with what apocryphal symbolisms this game corresponded to Chance.

Chance, Chance, the senator intoned to himself. No. No. Chance there is, but there are other forces, greater still. There is the will, there is the thrust, there is God. Destiny of men had never been a mere game of chance.

The heart of Samuel Harding beat more and more violently. Something was happening in his heart that resembled a short circuit, but fresh hope bloomed in him, fresh hope fashioned by faith and despair. And, as he was standing so, across from the young girl, on the other side of the table, Samuel bent over the green felt and said, tenderly and anxiously: "Adelaide?"

The young girl looked at him, answering with tears in her eyes:

"Yes...I am called Adelaide...I lost the game though." Wild joy made the heart of the senator jump. O miracle of miracles. The young girl was named Adelaide. Samuel's heart stirred in him like a tempestuous sea. This young girl was his, totally his — his daughter, his mistress and his wife. The young girl was the summit of his life.

"Adelaide. Adelaide. Don't cry....Don't feel sorry....We'll play again together and you'll win."

Saying this, the senator put his right hand in his

waistcoat pocket, and taking out of it as many five-dollar golden coins as it contained, threw them one by one, with incredible accuracy, like chip dealers in card games, into Adelaide's hands. And as the golden eagles and the trackers of prairies fell on the green table Samuel shouted in wild joy:

"Take these, my love, and play again...."

The beautiful young girl looked dazedly at the golden rain of coins before her. The senator looked at her with appealing ardor.

"Take them, my love, and play again....Play it all....Play until you win. I am here for you....I, Uncle Sam, in person."

At this point, the governess, recovering from her surprise, attempted to intervene.

"Thank you, but we've got money..." she said, opening her purse.

The senator thundered at her with scowling face.

"Keep your money, my good woman....Mine is different....It is made of my blood and soul. Keep your money, woman."

The governess retreated before him, dimly aware of the urgency of the occasion. Besides, the senator's erection remained fully visible.

Samuel turned to the young girl again. Adelaide's face was now radiant. All traces of sorrow had disappeared.

"Thank you....Thank you very much..." she said, and at once added:

"But, isn't all this money, so many golden dollars, too much. Each game costs only 20 cents."

"No, my beloved....I want you to play with all this..." Harding went on passionately. "And twice this if need be....And only with gold...for good luck...to have the fun of it together....So that you win and you will win....Do you hear, my little Adelaide?...I am telling you, you shall win...."

Adelaide glowed with joy. She took a golden coin with her white hand, placed it in the slot and after looking mischievously at Harding, pushed it in. Then she pulled the lever and the ball shot out.

Samuel had been deeply moved by looking at what the young girl had been doing there in front of him. At that moment, it seemed to him that he had become engaged to her.

The ball traveled, and Adelaide looked at it ecstatically. The senator stared at her, enslaved. The small metallic ball had already passed by nine stations.

"Salt Lake City," cried the girl jumping with joy, as the ball slid by the capital of the State of Utah.

The ball was approaching Carson City, the fatal city of Nevada, where it had shipwrecked the first time. For a moment, Harding shuddered. Adelaide grew pale and opened her round eyes in agony. Suddenly, they both cried at the same moment, in perfect unison.

"Nevada! Carson City!"

"We passed!" cried Adelaide.

"Yes. Yes....We passed..." cried Harding, too, in triumph, as the Argonauts would cry leaving the Symplegades behind them.

"We are approaching the Pacific!" cried the young girl convulsively.

"Yes, only one station to go, Sacramento, before we arrive, my love, at the end." Harding trembled.

Two or three seconds more and the young girl cried out:

"Sacramento. We have passed Sacramento!"

"Adelaide, you won. The next station is San Francisco! The Pacific! The greatest ocean in the world!"

Samuel's heart beat furiously. It now seemed to

him that he was no longer merely a human unit but a vast river-mouth over which flew, allies and brothers, the largest, the most glorious Colorado eagles. His joy was not simply joy but paradise. The ball had fallen in the ultimate hole and the model of the famous Pacific Railway Express, without warning, suddenly, thunder-like, was beginning on the triumphant round of the table, the triumphant round of the New World.

At the same moment, without warning, suddenly, thunder-like, Samuel Harding, the millionaire, consultant of the United Slaughter Houses of Chicago, vice-president of the Steam Navigation Transports of Lake Michigan, president of the Union Railways Company and senator of Illinois to the Congress, was falling dead but victorious, full of love, dollars and glory, at the feet of the blonde Adelaide, for ever father and lover of the girl, forever father and lover of the United States — the United States of all the World.

Indolence, whatever some may say, is a great evil. Not for moral reasons but for biological ones, for reasons that go beyond even the so-called existential philosophy.

I must explain myself. I feel it. So, there.

Once, on the outskirts of New Jerusalem (or Salt Lake City), there lived a red-blond-haired Mormon — Daniel Carter. This man had three beautiful wives — Penelope, Georgiana and Catherine. Daniel was good and kind. But he had one fault. He was lazy.

For the first three years of his conjugal life, everything went well. In the fourth year, he married two more wives — Ruth and Helen. Another year passed and still everything went well. Daniel, carefree and healthy, lived happily with his wives. But at the end of the fifth year a fire burned down the model tannery which he had inherited from his father and the kind Mormon lost everything except for a house and a few valuables. It was then that his indolence became manifest.

Penelope, who had more courage with him than his other wives, used to say to him often: "My dear

Dan, why don't you try to work, why don't you do something....We'll shrivel of poverty....We'll die of hunger...."

Now and then Dan sold something valuable, saying, as he caressed his long red-blond beard:

"God is merciful, God is merciful to good men."

The truth is that Daniel, besides being lazy, was a daydreamer as well. He believed in a happy Jerusalem eternally protected from above by the Almighty.

One day, Penelope tried him again:

"Listen Dan, I am telling you out of love. You must work. You may, perhaps, find it difficult for the first few days, but you will like it in the end. You are hale and strong. You are a brave man. Get it into your mind. You must work."

This time, Daniel Carter had second thoughts. It's true, he thought, Penelope is right. His beloved city was not only called New Jerusalem; it was also called Salt Lake City.

"All right," he told his wife, picking up his round, broad-rimmed hat. "All right, I'll go to the lake to think and tomorrow I will make up my mind."

"O, good, Dan!" his first wife exclaimed, tears in her eyes.

"So long," answered Daniel and went on his way towards the lake where he was particularly fond of sitting and daydreaming. On the way he kept repeating over and over again, and for the first time in his life with some bitterness:

"Jerusalem! Jerusalem! O, my salty city!"

An hour later Daniel Carter was sitting under a tree on the lake shore, his chin in his hands, wondering what he ought to do.

It was a beautiful spring day. The water, always salty, seemed to be very sweet. The hills opposite were covered with grass and spotted all over with cows. Near the entrance to a farm a girl was milking a cow.

Not far away from Carter a placid-looking fellow wearing a straw hat was patiently fishing and smoking a pipe.

Daniel, preoccupied, gazed at the landscape. Eventually his attention focused on the girl milking the cow.

His thoughts became daydreams; the daydreams became visions and the visions ecstatic contemplations.

He could become a farmer. He could also add this beautiful girl to his collection of wives. He could gradually become a big landowner and, at the same time, an apostle of the Mormon faith throughout the world. He could easily end up President of the United States....Why not? Hadn't Abraham Lincoln started off a simple man?

But why was he saying: "I could become this or that?" He was already all these things. The young girl milking the cows became his wife. The day was superb. The fields were grassy. Everything was wonderful. God was great and his creation admirable!

"Jerusalem! Jerusalem! Beloved city!" the Mormon cried out passionately, rising to his feet. "New days shall come! New prophets shall come! I, Daniel, shall come to proclaim you, O, New Jerusalem, capital of the entire world, in the heart of Utah, on the shores of the beautiful lake!"

Uttering this invocation, the red-blond-haired Mormon walked towards the girl who was still milking the cows. He was powerful and glorious. He was all-powerful and a reformer of the Universe....

The man fishing near him on the lake-shore

nodded and thought: "Another madman....The world has gone mad." The young girl, seeing the ecstatic man advancing on her, left her cows and shut herself up in her home.

But Daniel was not disappointed. He was Carter, the Mormon, the great lover and reformer of the World. The same day he built an improvised cabin with leaves and branches and settled there, on the shores of the Salt Lake, on the outskirts of New Jerusalem. He revealed his love to the girl from a distance, continually enriching his visions.

On the third day he managed to approach the girl. On the fifth day, he married her. On the sixth day — perhaps because this girl was his sixth wife — he remembered that the others had been waiting for him, Penelope, Georgiana, Catherine, Ruth and Helen. So he took Caroline — that was the name of his new wife — set fire to the improvised cabin and anxiously returned home.

What had happened to his other wives? Had they, perhaps, gone? Had they died? Had they been begging for bread in the streets while he was again performing new nuptial celebrations?

An unwelcome sight awaited him there. Two cattle-dealers, a money-changer, the proprietor of a gambling house and a vulgar agitator had set themselves up in his home and, having made his five wives their concubines, were amusing themselves for a piece of bread....And he who was returning from the lake, his new wife at his side, to announce the joyful news that a new era was starting, that he had decided to work, was left standing there like a cuckold at the door of his own home.

It was then that there suddenly awoke in Daniel's heart the blood of the old immigrants, the blood of the Puritan adventurers. Before his eyes shone the handsome face of the arch-Mormon, Joseph Smith. Daniel Carter suddenly became a man of action. In the twinkling of an eye, he had whipped two six-barrel revolvers (Smith-Wessons) from their holsters, shooting them in the air. The five suitors took to their heels, rushing toward the open windows, while the terrified women, clasping their hands, stretched them entreatingly towards their husband.

But Daniel had no intention of letting the five men get away unpunished. Uttering terrible curses he fired the two pistols incessantly. One after the other the suitors hurled themselves from the window, falling to the grass with bullets in their buttocks, while the six wives of the Mormon knelt at his feet kissing them.

A year later, Daniel became a dealer in wild horses. Two years later he became mayor of Salt Lake City and five years later a thick book, under the following name and title, appeared in all the bookshop windows of New Jerusalem:

DANIEL CARTER

The return of Ulysses
or
the glory of the Mormons

GREEN INTEGER
Pataphysics and Pedantry

Douglas Messerli, *Publisher*

Essays, Manifestos, Statements, Speeches, Maxims,
Epistles, Diaristic Notes, Narratives, Natural Histories,
Poems, Plays, Performances, Ramblings, Revelations
and all such ephemera as may appear necessary
to bring society into a slight tremolo of confusion
and fright at least.

MASTERWORKS OF FICTION

Masterworks of Fiction is a program of Green Integer to reprint
important works of fiction from all centuries. We make no claim to any
superiority of these fictions over others in either form or subject, but
rather we contend that these works are highly enjoyable to read and,
more importantly, have challenged the ideas and language of the times
in which they were published, establishing themselves over the years as
among the outstanding works of their period. By republishing both well
known and lesser recognized titles in this series we hope to continue our
mission bringing our society into a slight tremolo of confusion and
fright at least.

BOOKS IN THIS SERIES

José Donoso *Hell Has No Limits* (1966)
Knut Hamsun *A Wanderer Plays on Muted Strings* (1909)
Raymond Federman *The Twofold Vibration* (1982)

Gertrude Stein *To Do: A Book of Alphabets
and Birthdays* (1957)
Gérard de Nerval *Aurélia* (1855)
Tereza Albues *Pedra Canga* (1987)
Sigurd Hoel *Meeting at the Milestone* (1947)
Leslie Scalapino *Defoe* (1994)
Charles Dickens *A Christmas Carol* (1843)
Anthony Powell *O, How the Wheel Becomes It!* (1983)
Ole Sarvig *The Sea Below My Window* (1960)
Anthony Powell *Venusburg* (1932)
Arthur Schnitzler *Lieutenant Gustl* (1900)
Andreas Embiricos *Amour Amour* (1960)
Toby Olson *Utah* (1987)

*

Green Integer Books

Amour Amour   Andreas Embiricos

Translated from the Greek by Nikos Stangos and Alan Ross.
With an Introduction by Nanos Valaoritis

In this book of twenty-four stories, or "personal mythologies," Greek novelist and poet Andreas Embiricos combines history, myth, poetry, and psychology to create a sensual, original and fabulous universe. His characters, defying all convention, behave like the ancient gods in their often murderous and pleasure-seeking expeditions, fulfilling instincts latent in everyone.

Born in 1901, Andreas Embiricos worked in the offices of the London-based Byron Steamship Company (which belonged to his family) between 1921 and 1925. He later moved to Paris, where he joined the surrealist group of André Breton. Among his many books are **Blast Furnace** and **Argo**, or **The Voyage of a Balloon**. **Amour Amour** was published in Greece as **Grapta** (Writings) in 1960.

GREEN INTEGER 87 $

ISBN 1-931243-26-3
51195

9 781931 243261

FICTION/GREEK LITERATURE